LET HIM STAY

THE NATEXUS SERIES

VICKI JAMES

COVER DESIGN:

Lou J Stock of L.J. Designs.

EDITED BY:

Claire Allmendinger of BNW Editing.

PROMOTIONS:

Wendy Shatwell and Claire Allmendinger of Bare Naked Words.

www.barenakedwords.co.uk

DEDICATED TO:

My husband.
In case I don't tell you enough... I love you.

PART THREE

THE TIME AFTER IT BEGAN AGAIN

"There I was, way off my ambitions, getting deeper in love every minute, and all of a sudden I didn't care."

F. SCOTT FITZGERALD, THE GREAT GATSBY

ONE

Alexander Law was now my reality.

My cheeks ached when we arrived in London. I'd been goofy in my adoration of his face, making sure to take in every single detail I could while he sat beside me with his hand on my thigh and our shoulders pressed together. It didn't escape my notice that my happy memories of Alex tended to start with a journey on a bus, and this was no different. I felt like a child at Christmas, the excitement for this next chapter untameable.

But I couldn't lie to myself; I was also nervous.

I'd dreamed of Alex and me walking out into the open air without fear, uncertainty or a dark cloud of grief and mistrust hanging over our heads. I'd just never had the courage to prepare myself for how I would feel when he turned to face me before taking my hand in his and guiding me out into the streets of our new adventure.

I froze at the small gesture, feeling the way his fingers curled around mine protectively. I glanced down to where our hands were clasped together, and the smile that broke free soon ached.

"I like that smile."

I looked back up at him. "I'm happy."

He didn't even try to hide his relief. It was only fleeting, a small second of uncertainty that was quickly drowned out by what was to follow: elation. His eyes lit up like fireworks, and his grin grew high and bright. Leaning down, he cupped my cheek with his palm. It was like looking into a mirror and seeing a perfect reflection of everything I was feeling inside.

I *was* happy. This was what it felt like.

"This is just the start." He pressed his lips to mine, and there we were, kissing the first kiss of our time in London together.

We'd always been Natexus, even when we'd been apart, but now it was time to go all the way standing side by side.

The possibilities suddenly seemed endless.

"Are you ready?" I asked as I pulled away.

Alex's eyes flickered open and he sucked in a breath while I stared at the perfection of him and tried to ignore the goosebumps that rose on the back of my neck.

"So ready," he whispered.

Alex grinned, dropping his fingers from my cheek as he turned to grab hold of my suitcase beside him. He never let go of my hand as we both turned to look at the bustling streets.

"Look at this, Nat. There's a whole world of new things out there waiting for us. All those possibilities, all those firsts for us to experience together…"

"I think I know where we should go first," I said over the noise of the traffic.

"Where?"

"Our hotel room."

"To dump our things?"

"No." I shook my head. "To bed."

"Are you tired?"

"Nope." I grinned.

"Then, what... oh." Alex's mouth stayed in that adorable 'O' shape for some time, his eyes practically popping out of his head. "Oh," he repeated slowly. "Christ. Shit. Yeah. Let's do that. Let's go."

I barely had time to blink before Alex had his arm in the air, flagging down the nearest taxi he could find before throwing our bags into the boot of the cab with a force that was unnecessary but incredibly charming, nonetheless. When he eventually dived into the back seat, he barked instructions at the driver to get us to the hotel as quickly as possible.

It took us twenty minutes to get there because of the traffic, and I was certain Alex touched every part of me he could that was above my clothes in the back of that taxi. It was the longest twenty minutes of our lives.

But I knew it was going to be worth the wait when we got there.

The entire five years had been worth the wait.

Truth was, I'd have waited my whole damn life to love him how I was loving him now if I'd had to. He was who I had been destined for, and when we walked into our room, throwing our bags into a corner before he backed me up to stand over our bed, all I could do was thank every god that existed that they'd let me have him sooner rather than later.

I was breathing freely again. I was flying high.

Just like those birds we used to talk about.

TWO

I was twenty-two, and my fears about my own body had long since died. Deep down, I guess I knew that I had my ex-boyfriend Marcus to thank for that. But, no matter how many times I'd gone to bed with him, or how many times I'd replayed the night I first made love to Alex in my mind, nothing could have ever prepared me for the way I felt the moment the backs of my legs hit the mattress of that bed in our London hotel room.

The air felt incredibly thin, and my vision went hazy as I held on tightly to Alex's shoulders and looked up into his eyes. I couldn't breathe—couldn't think or do anything other than wait for him to make a move that would stop my body and mind from freefalling.

"Everything okay?"

"Perfect," I squeaked, quickly clearing my throat.

He smirked seductively, moving both his hands from my hips up to the middle of my spine. "Natalie Vincent, are you…?"

"Don't say it."

"Nervous?" he whispered.

"Damn it, Alex." I sighed. I really didn't want to be the scared little schoolgirl he remembered me as. I wanted to be new, confident, and to show him how he never had to worry about breaking or hurting me again.

"Sweetheart, I can feel you trembling. Your knees are knocking together so hard they sound like coconuts."

"Maybe it's your coconuts that are knocking together. Maybe it's you who's scared."

"There's no air between those right now. Trust me. The only sound they're making might be a weak mewling from their suffocation."

"Oh my God." I chuckled, slowly closing my eyes to compose myself.

What was wrong with me? Why was I acting this way? This was everything I'd ever wanted. *He* was all I'd ever wanted. Now I had him right where I'd always dreamed of him being, and I was turning into a hot mess in the blink of an eye.

"Breathe, Natalie," he whispered softly to me before blowing a small stream of air over my face, forcing my eyes to flutter open. If he was trying to get me even higher from just the smell of him, it worked. I was dizzy, my head spinning. "Breathe," he repeated. "It's just me."

"You say that like you're no big deal."

"I'm not."

"Easy for you to say. You don't have to look at you."

"No, I have to look at *you*. That's a much bigger deal."

"I'm sorry," I muttered in embarrassment. "I don't know

what's wrong with me."

"This is the biggest moment of our lives. It's what we've both been dreaming of for years, right?"

"Right." I exhaled again, sliding my hands around the back of his neck carefully.

"And you just want it to be perfect."

"Beyond perfect."

"And you're panicking about whether it will ever feel as good as the first time we made love."

"I am?"

He nodded gently, his eyes falling to my lips as he spoke again. "That night was incredible. I've never had a night like that since, and a part of me knows we'll never find those exact feelings again."

"Oh…" My face fell, and I tried not to sound disappointed, but Alex's eyes were soon staring back into mine, his face alive with amusement and excitement.

"I don't want to go back to what we had, Nat," he began. "That night with you was the best night of my life, but I want us to go forward and create something new now—something neither of us has ever felt or experienced before. I want us to stop looking back, to stop thinking about the past. I want us to make new memories. I want us to be twenty-two together and screw like twenty-two-year-olds do."

The colour of fire rushed to my cheeks, my stomach quickly flipping in excitement as I squeezed my thighs together.

"Shit," he said with a laugh. "I want us to stay in bed for seven days, only getting out to shower, order room service, or use the bathroom. I want us to laugh at four o'clock in the morning over stupid things. I want us to fall asleep at two in the afternoon just because we have nowhere else to be. I want to find out everything about you—every moment I've missed—and I want you to help me figure out who I am again because I swear you know me more than I have ever known myself."

My grin was ridiculous as I raised both brows and watched him watching me.

"More than anything, I want to make so many amazing memories with you that the first time we made love won't even sit in the top one hundred happiest moments of our lives together when we're old and grey. I'm going to make you so happy, Nat. You've just got to let me."

"I'll let you," I whispered.

"But…" Alex's small growl rumbled in the back of his throat before he moved his hands back down to my waist and slowly began to peel himself away until there was an inch of space between us. "I'm not going to rush this first time with you."

"What? Get back here. I'm fine," I croaked, immediately cursing myself for sounding anything *but* fine. "I'm fine," I tried again, sounding even worse. "Goddamn it." I reached up to wiggle my throat, opening my mouth as I rolled my jaw around.

He scowled playfully, trying to peek into my mouth. "You got a frog stuck down there or something?"

"I'hink I'av," I strained out.

"Let me see if I can help you out." Alex curled his hand around mine, pulling it away from my throat before he cupped my jaw in both hands.

His kiss was exactly what I needed, an instant cure to dilute the pressure I felt to make this moment more perfect than it already was. And, despite the ache between my legs that was crying out for me to get a grip of myself and throw him down on the bed, I decided that he was, in fact, right. I was too nervous for this to happen right now. I needed a shower after the long journey. I needed to hold his hand some more, feel his chest under my palms, stare into his eyes and study his face after years of being apart. I needed just a little bit more time to pinch myself and realise that this was really real. I could give myself that. I could give myself anything now in this new life I was about to dive into.

THREE

"What are you doing?" he asked with amusement, watching me as I fussed around the hotel room. Alex was lying on the bed, his arms tucked behind his head while I tried not to focus on the bare patch of skin that was showing around his stomach where his shirt had ridden up.

"I'm distracting myself."

"From?"

"Thinking."

"About?"

"You."

"You're adorable, Vincent." His laughter was rough, lazy, relaxed.

My cheeks flamed again, and I internally chastised my body for the way it was bickering with my heart to harden up. It wanted a release—an Alex Law induced release—but I had a plan, and that plan was to unpack the bags, settle in, and make this place somewhat cosy for the next ten days. The Landmark London Hotel was something I was certain I would never experience again. The room we were staying in was more like an apartment, and the only reason I was able to afford such fine surroundings was thanks to my parents helping me to fund this trip, wanting me to stay in places they knew weren't homeless shelters. Both Mum and Dad wanted to keep me safe. At first, I'd told them I couldn't accept it, but once my father had given me 'that' look, I conceded and let them spoil me. Apparently, he knew someone who used to be a porter at the hotel, meaning there had been a few strings pulled to get me in at such short notice.

The room was spacious and light. The king-sized bed hugged only half of the back wall, and the interior of the whole place was pale mint and blue running alongside warm welcoming cream and gold. Sitting by the huge bay windows that overlooked London was a coffee table with two small sofas on either side, and a pile of highbrow magazines stacked on top.

It was a surprise to me that I saw as many details of the place as I did. The only thing I had been focused on since we pushed through the door was Alex.

I was fussing and I knew it. Within thirty minutes, I'd unpacked my bag, placed my toiletries in the bathroom and brushed my hair approximately seven hundred and forty-two times, until I had nothing left to do but turn and face him again.

He hadn't moved. His gaze had followed me around the room. I could feel it burning holes of lust into my skin, much the same way they had done at Suzie and Paul's wedding, only this time there was no guilt attached to him undressing me with his eyes.

Get it together, Nat.

"Hi." I smiled pathetically and turned to face him.

Alex closed his eyes as his laughter poured free. He pushed himself upright before he crawled across the mattress, rising up on his knees at the end of the bed.

"Come here," he instructed, holding out his hand.

I took it slowly, pressing my lips together when he pulled me closer and curled both of his arms around my waist. I held onto his biceps, leaning back against his strong arms so I could see as much of him as possible.

"Want to know something?" he asked. "I think I'm actually more nervous about this than you are."

"Oh, I doubt that."

"Natalie, the last time I was in a hotel room with you, you walked away from me, and I thought I'd never get the chance to do anything more with you than spend my life jogging past your house and catching glimpses of you from afar." Alex shot a single finger up to my lips before I could protest. "I'm not telling you this for us to go back over everything again. Remember, we're living for today. I'm just trying to explain to you that I've spent years dreaming about this moment and now that it's here, I'm terrified I'm going to fuck this up."

"I'm overthinking everything, aren't I?" I mumbled behind his finger, forcing him to drop his hand back to my waist.

"Definitely overthinking." He nodded enthusiastically, and I wanted to sink my teeth into that smirking mouth of his just to show him who was boss. My stomach flipped at the thought, and I could feel the trembling of my knees begin to rumble beneath me. "But I can wait. I will wait. You never have to do anything just to make someone else happy, ever, ever again."

I took that as my cue to close the gap and kiss him. There wasn't anything in the world that compared to the feel of him against my lips. Alex wasn't your average twenty-two-year-old. His mind was wiser, his hands felt rougher, his jaw was strong, and his eyes held an extraordinary amount of life and awareness in them. But his lips… oh, his lips. They were the most sensuous experience I'd ever had—a perfect combination of soft yet firm. The control was always there, but the movements and the sweep of his tongue across mine made me melt in his arms until it felt like my eyes were rolling into the back of my head.

"There's my girl," he whispered against my mouth when I moaned. "There's my Natalie."

"I'm your Natalie." My voice was quiet but confident, and my hands roamed up to his shoulders, my fingers spreading as I dragged my nails into the small curve of his neck before moving around to tug on the ends of his hair. "And you're my Alex."

"Every inch of me is yours."

I could feel the goosebumps rising at the nape of his neck, and with every visible reaction he gave me, I grew stronger and more assured that waiting any longer was nothing short of stupid.

I leaned forward, hovering my lips only an inch away from his ear before whispering, "Natexus."

"All the way, baby," he mouthed, while his fingers curled into the back of my shirt with no tenderness at all.

I grinned, and then I pushed Alex back onto the mattress with as much force as I could. His body bounced, his legs flying out underneath him. When his eyes popped open and met mine, I stood there in front of him and began to unbutton my shirt, making sure I never looked away. His gaze fell, dropping to where I was opening each button as slowly as I could manage.

It didn't take me long to remove my jeans, and when my fingers went to unclip my bra, Alex's hand shot up in the air urgently.

"No," he called out, a little breathless.

I tilted my head to one side and raised a brow. "No?"

"Let me do it," he begged. "Let me do the rest. You have no idea how long I've been waiting to undress you."

I took that as my cue to join him. Climbing onto the bed until I was straddling Alex's waist, my bare thighs stroking against his jeans, I eventually leaned down and pressed my chest to his.

Alex's hands found my hair and pushed it back over my shoulders with a tenderness that screamed of his adoration for me. "I love you."

"I know, but say it again… one more time."

"I love you."

I closed my eyes to let myself drown in those three words before I looked at him again and grinned. "I love you."

"And I'm about to turn your whole world upside down."

"Again?" I whispered.

"With brute force."

"God, I hope so," I breathed out shamelessly.

His erection was taunting me, pressing against the lower parts of my stomach that were tight with desperate need and desire. I knew we could go back and forth all night long, but all I wanted, all I craved, was to feel him inside me.

As if reading my mind, Alex bucked his hips slowly, riding his arse against the bed in a hypnotic rhythm until we were both working together to create more friction against one another. His hands found the backs of my thighs before they began to make their way up my body at a frustrating pace. They seemed to go everywhere. My skin was caressed, gently scratched, grabbed and soothed over and over again, and his fingers only ever skimmed under the edges of my underwear, not allowing themselves to explore any further just yet. I knew what he was doing. He was soaking it in, taking his time. He was being gentle before he unleashed himself on me, luring me into a false sense of security before he made his mark on my body.

My kisses were greedy as I lost myself in the myriad of sensations that were running through me. I was handing everything I had over to Alex for the first time ever without any reservations or fears of what the aftermath would bring. There wasn't sadness or heartache in our eyes this time, just pure need and excitement with a touch of disbelief causing our smiles to occasionally bump against one another or interrupt the kiss.

While my breathing became louder—the quiet mewls of appreciation falling freely now—Alex's breaths became heavy and dark. Every brush of my touch over his erection made his growls turn more desperate, until the final stroke had his hands flying to my bra and practically ripping it from my back. With every second that passed us by, we were losing the tenderness of our reunion, and the only thing that either of us had in the very depths of our stomachs was fire. It was a fire that was going to burn us alive if we didn't try to contain it. A fire that neither one of us had any desire to keep under control, because after too long apart, it was obvious that Natexus would happily burn together before separating ever again.

The second he ripped my thong from me, snapping it in two with ease, Alex stepped up a gear. His fingers dug into my waist before he lifted me off him and flipped me onto my back, so I was lying beneath him, naked and unashamed.

He jumped from the bed and shrugged out of his clothes with no grace or apologies. Never once did his eyes leave my body. There was a hunger in them that I'd never seen before.

As soon as he stepped out of his underwear and climbed back on top, I hitched in a breath and held it high in my chest. Alex hovered above me, the strength in his shoulders and biceps making my stomach flip again. His knees slowly began to nudge my legs apart, and with one hand, he pushed my arms above my head and kept them captive at the wrists.

"Is this Heaven?" he whispered through a small, devilish smile.

"Heaven wishes it was this good."

When he began to drop kisses to my cheeks, slowly making his way down my neck before marking every single inch of my body with his tongue, I sank into a world of sex I'd never discovered before that night. It was animal needs mixed with a love so powerful it felt strong enough to kill me, and the only thought I had was how it would be the most blessed way to go.

FOUR

It took two days for Alex to convince me that we should leave our room and at least attempt to see the great city of London. It took a lot of kisses for him to convince me that there could be anything out there worth looking at that would ever compare to him.

"This is why you're here, Nat," he would say through that knowing smile of his. "You wanted to go discover yourself, to discover the world. Just because I've tagged along it doesn't mean that's going to stop."

My petulant pouts only lasted a couple of seconds before he did something in true Alex Law fashion to make me forget any kind of upset.

He was right, of course. As soon as we'd stepped out into the real world and allowed ourselves to be caught up in the buzz of that vibrant city, we came to life together. Natexus was no longer dormant, just a thing we both used to speak of. It was alive, pulsing and growing stronger with every second that we held hands, kissed or laughed together. It was maturing, and the heartbeat of what we were when we were side by side often seemed so loud and so visible, I could have sworn people could see it hanging over us like a giant cartoon love heart that followed us around, wearing a smile on its face while sighing happily. *It's happened. They're together. Ring all the church bells and tell everybody to dance in the streets!*

For the first time since I'd met him, everything about Alex was lighter than air. Gone were his frown lines and that unsure look in his eyes. Gone were the tense jaw and the constant forced smiles. In London, his grin was dazzling and bright.

We visited many places together, taking photographs at any given opportunity. He wanted to make sure he captured every memory, and I knew that even though we were having the time of our lives, there was a part of him that thought it was all too good to be true.

Outside Buckingham Palace, we tried to make the guards laugh, and I listened as Alex yelled ridiculously bad jokes at them, not caring who was looking. We clung to the gates, and we posed by the statue, asking passers-by to take pictures. Alex even bought me a blow-up crown and forced me to wear it for the entire afternoon, telling me I looked adorable, even though I knew I looked a fool.

On the London Eye, we rose high in the sky as the sun began to set, and we kissed the entire way around, only occasionally stopping when it felt like our breaths were running out and our jaws were going to fall off.

We saw two stage shows in The West End, but despite my tears, which flowed freely from the hypnotic music alone, I spent most of my time watching Alex from the corner of my eyes rather than paying attention to the actual actors in *Wicked* or *Les Misérables*.

We ate in small pubs, overdosing on food and indulging in wine, losing ourselves in each other's company until we didn't have a clue what time of day it was anymore. The only thing we cared about was hearing each other's voices and enjoying our very own version of middle city paradise.

The souvenir shops made a small fortune from us. There just didn't seem to be enough of them to invade. From tacky ornaments for Suzie and Paul's new home to seventeen different postcards for my parents, and Union Jack wigs that I forced him to wear the whole way back to our hotel room—we bought it all, laughing the entire time. Alex showered me with so many gifts, some days it was a struggle for me to accept them. But the look on his face whenever he surprised me with something that made me smile was my own reward. He looked happy. He *was* happy.

Time passed quickly. I wasn't even aware what day it was when we were sauntering down the street hand in hand and Alex quickly veered off to the left, pulling me into yet another souvenir shop.

My head fell back, and I allowed a small groan to rumble in the depths of my throat. "Another one? Alex, I'm pretty sure we own every tacky ornament London has to offer. Our hotel room is overflowing with red, white and blue."

He rolled his eyes and his smile grew bigger. "This is the last thing. I promise."

inside of the store was the same as most of the others. Lining the walls were row upon row of T-shirts, vests, jumpers and bags. Anywhere a vendor could stick another item to sell, they did. No space was unusable.

Alex raised his chin as he approached the lady at the cash

register. The look he gave her was one that told me this wasn't exactly their first meeting, yet I couldn't figure out a time when he'd have been able to sneak in here without me.

"Hi," Alex started. "I'm here to pick up those things I ordered."

The young woman was stunning, with jet-black hair that fell to her waist and bright blue eyes that shone vividly under the harsh lighting of the store. She could have had anyone she wanted; she probably did, but that didn't stop her cheeks from blushing or her chest expanding the second she took one look up into Alex's eyes.

It was understandable. I did the same thing. But even though I could appreciate the effect he had on the world, there was always a small flicker of jealousy that washed over me whenever I saw someone react to him that way. It was an emotion I'd never felt with Marcus, and that wasn't lost on me.

"Ah, hello again, Mr Law. They're right here for you, just as you requested."

My hand gripped his tighter, and Alex turned to face me, looking me straight in the eyes before flashing me a wink of reassurance.

I forced myself to look at the sales assistant, and I watched as she bent down to collect a package from underneath the till before she placed it on the counter carefully.

"Okay, here it is. There are two—like you ordered," she told him. "Just double-check that the sizes are right, and you're good to go."

"I'm sure they're perfect. No need for me to check anything." Alex pulled his hand away from mine to collect the package before scooping it under one arm while digging in his pocket with his free hand for something else. "I can't thank you enough for rushing this through for me."

The assistant tucked her hair behind her ear before waving

him off. "Really. It was no bother."

"It was. Your mother told me that you usually take a few days to do these, so I appreciate you spending your time to help me make my girl smile. You're trying to save up to go travelling, right?"

"Erm." She blinked quickly as if caught off guard before she nodded and corrected herself. "That's right. My mum told you that?"

"She's incredibly proud of you. I hear good parents who love their children as much as she seems to love you make that known to anybody who will listen."

She blushed, a small frown flickering across her face before she looked down at the counter, clearly embarrassed. "Thank you."

Alex smiled flatly at her before he pulled out a twenty-pound note from his pocket, sliding it across the counter smoothly. "No. Thank you."

"You've already paid. There's nothing outstanding on this bill."

"I know." He smiled. "This is for you. Every little bit helps, right? And like I said, I appreciate you sorting this order out for me."

The woman's hand reached out for the tip, and her eyes glazed over for a second before she took it in both hands and rolled it around. "Thank you," she mouthed again.

After a further few small exchanges, Alex turned back to me and began to guide me out of the shop. I let him take the lead, casting one last glimpse over my shoulder at the young woman who was now wiping a tear away from her cheek, not knowing I was watching.

When we stepped back outside and a cool chill wrapped itself around my arms, I finally spoke.

"She was crying," I told him quietly.

"Who was?"

"The girl who just served you. As we were leaving, I looked back at her and she was crying."

"She's probably not used to people tipping her." He smirked, shuffling the package farther under his arm.

My attention fell to it immediately before I narrowed my eyes and looked back up at him. "You're up to something. What's in the package, Alex?"

He stopped in his tracks and pulled it out in front of him, rolling it around in his hands before he looked up at me and held it out.

"Don't get too excited. This is just a bit of fun."

I took the package gingerly, never breaking eye contact with him as I felt the softness of it in my hands. "Oh, good. For a moment there, I thought you were about to surprise me with a giant blow-up engagement ring or something."

His face faltered for just a second. "An engagement ring?"

My cheeks flamed to life. "It was a joke, Alex. I didn't... I mean, I... You don't... I don't want..."

His laughter broke the tension quickly "Just open the package, baby. There's nothing scary inside. There's nothing life-changing."

I did as I was told while taking a few calming breaths to allow myself to focus. The paper fell to my feet as I unwrapped it until I was left holding two hoodies, one in each hand.

"Hoodies?" I said with surprise.

"See. Nothing scary," he whispered. "Open them up."

I handed him the black one while I opened up the purple one and held it out by the shoulders. Down the front in giant letters were the words I Love London. A huge smile broke out on my face as I read it, but what I didn't see straight away were the smaller words that were written in italics between the bigger ones. My eyes scanned the fabric over and over until the message he'd had embroidered on the front shone out like a neon sign.

"**I** *fell in* **LOVE** *all over again in* **LONDON**." The words came out in a whisper as I dropped the hoodie down to see his face. "Alex…"

"Turn it around," he instructed, his eyes alive with excitement.

I did as he asked and looked at the back, reading the words 'All the way, baby' embroidered in the most beautiful italic script.

"You had this made for me?"

"Your very own personalised piece of crappy London tat."

My eyes shot up to his. "This could never be crappy or tat. This is the most amazing—"

Alex leaned forward to cut me off with a kiss, his lips pressing firmly to mine and causing my eyes to close, just for a second, while I soaked him up. When he pulled away and I let my eyes flicker open, my grin rose to match his.

"Sorry. I saw that look on your face and I had to kiss you. I promised myself I'd never hold back again whenever I got that urge."

"You never have to apologise for interrupting me with a kiss." I rubbed my smiling lips together and looked down at the gift still in my hands before glancing back up at him. "I love that you did this for me." Curling the material up in my fists, I pressed it to my chest and let out a small, nervous laugh. "What does the other hoodie say?"

"Oh, this one?" He held it out and showed me the back, which had the same cursive 'All the way, baby' in white across it. "This one is for me."

"You got us matching hoodies?" I chuckled.

His mouth pulled up at one side as he pretended to cringe. "Kinda. Is that cheesy?"

"Totally cheesy."

"That's why I had mine done a little differently."

"What does yours say?" I waited as he turned it around and allowed me to see the front.

As soon as the words came into focus, I threw my head back and let out the biggest shriek of laughter I had within me. "You didn't!" I cried.

"What?" He grinned, his shoulders bouncing as his own laughter poured free.

"Alex, there's no way in Hell you are going to wear that in public."

"You wanna bet?" he challenged, his brows rising high on his forehead before he threw the hoodie over his head and pushed his arms inside. When he pulled it down over his chest, the words shone proudly for the world to see.

"**I** *fell in* **LOVE** *with being my girlfriend's sex slave in* **LONDON**," I read out to him, shaking my head as the laughter made my body shake. "What will people think?"

"Isn't that why we're down here, Nat? We're learning not to care what anyone thinks of us."

"Alex?"

"Yes, babe?"

I took a step closer and lifted a hand to the embroidery on his hoodie. My finger traced over the word girlfriend a dozen times before I eventually looked up at him through my lashes and grinned.

"I'm your girlfriend."

His hands circled my waist and he pulled me closer before dropping his forehead to mine. "Damn right."

"I guess this means I can do anything I want with you? I can ask anything I want of you?"

"If you don't already know the answer to that by now, I don't know what the hell else to do to show you."

When I kissed him, I believed it. I believed nothing could ever ruin what we had or try to come between us ever again. We'd been through so much and faced a lifetime of wrongs. How could we possibly have any other battles left to fight?

It was naive of me, but I basked in that naivety for as long as I could until I was forced to face reality. When that time came, I wasn't sure how I would survive without this bubble of contentment and happiness around me.

FIVE

"**W**e need to talk."

Alex had just showered and was making his way over to our bed with just a white towel wrapped around his waist while droplets of water trickled slowly down his chest. But those words he said made me lose all focus as I blinked up at him and lowered the book I was reading into my lap.

"About what?" I croaked.

Leaning down, Alex kissed me on the forehead before he sat on the mattress in front of me, one leg hitched up while the other dangled down to the floor.

"Us. This." Alex smiled softly. "The fact that you haven't spoken to your parents in days because you've been too busy with me."

"Oh." I paused. "Oh."

"Oh," he repeated. "I love this hideaway we've created for ourselves, but remember what happens when we keep ourselves in those bubbles, Nat."

"I know, I know." I sighed slowly, eventually tilting my head to one side. "I know we can't stay hidden away forever. I know it's not realistic. I mean… it's not like I've completely shut everyone off. I've been texting them to let them know I'm safe."

"Your parents. Yeah, okay. I'll give you that. What about Sammy?"

"What about Sammy?" I scowled.

"She's your best friend, and I've not heard you say more than ten words about her in the last seven days."

"Need I remind you that I've been a little preoccupied with a tall, dark, handsome young man?"

"No reminders needed." He smirked. "I do need to know one thing, though. Have I caused a rift between you guys? She's Marcus's sister. You were with him, and now you're not because of me. I know that must have put a strain on that guilt chip of yours."

"Sam has been fine with me about splitting up with Marcus. We spoke before I met you in the park that day. We spoke before I left to come down to London."

"But?"

"I don't know. It's different now."

"Different how?"

I pressed my lips together and let my shoulders sag in defeat. "Fine. You're right. I can't help but feel like I've let her down."

"I thought as much," he said quietly before he gripped the end of my chin between his thumb and finger. "But if I know Sammy, and I think I do, I know enough to be one hundred percent certain that she would want you to be the happiest you can be, no matter who you're with."

"She would. She does," I whispered back. "I just don't want to throw how happy I am in her face when I don't know how Marcus is coping with our break-up."

"Which brings me to my next point."

"Uh-oh."

"Maybe you should speak to Marcus, too."

I frowned harder, searching his eyes for some kind of jealousy at even the thought of me speaking to my ex again, but there wasn't anything there but certainty.

"You'd be happy with me speaking to Marcus?"

It was his turn to scowl. "You think I want you two to stop being friends?"

"I... don't... know..." I stuttered. "I just assumed..."

"Don't do that," he said with a shy grin. "The whole assuming thing making an arse of you and me thing." He let his hand fall from my face and into my lap where he curled his fingers around mine. "It's awkward. It's how we mess things up before we start, right?"

"Okay, where is Alex and what have you done with him?"

"What do you mean?" He laughed.

"I mean who the hell are you?" My grin was bright as I tugged on the end of his arm and silently beckoned him closer. "And why weren't you around when we were seventeen, all confident and bright, intelligent and wise?"

"I was just growing into my awesomeness back then. It took me a while."

"It was worth the wait," I whispered.

"So... Marcus?"

I sighed again, heavier this time, and gave him a small nod. "I'll call him."

"And Sammy?"

"I'll call her, too."

"And your parents?"

I nodded harder, half rolling my eyes at him before correcting myself and smirking. "And my parents."

"Good girl, baby." Alex leaned closer and went to place a kiss on the end of my nose, but I stopped him, reaching up to grip his chin the same way he'd done with mine. He froze in place, his lips only an inch away, and his minty breaths washing over me.

"In return, you're going to do a favour for me."

"Anything you want."

"Call your dad and check in on him. He's *your* family, and while I know you're putting yourself first for once, I also know that, deep down, you're hoping he's okay."

Alex's face hardened for the first time since we'd arrived in London, and I saw the blackness flash through his eyes and the tension return to his jaw. In a few flutters of his lashes, his worry and his anger had aged him significantly, making him seem much older than his actual years. I held my position, remaining soft as I stared into his eyes.

"You need this. *We* need this."

"Nat..."

"Please," I mouthed almost inaudibly. "For me."

In the blink of an eye, his uncertainty seemed to drift away. "Okay." He nodded. "For you."

"Thank you," I whispered, letting go of his chin before gifting him with a small kiss of reassurance. If he was going to make sure I didn't live a lie from now on, I was going to make sure I did the same for him.

Although our time here together had been perfect, I needed him to know that it wouldn't always have to stay this way for me to love him. It wouldn't always have to be this amazing for me to be by his side.

I wanted him for always.

Through the good, through the bad, and through every shade of ugly our two worlds could throw at us.

***

I ended the Skype call to Mum and Dad, feeling myself relax. They'd never looked happier, waving at Alex and me through the screen and asking about our adventures. Even Dad looked invested, while Mum cooed endlessly about how beautiful I looked. I hadn't known I'd needed to see them like that, and while I smiled at the blank screen, Alex ran a finger up my arm as he laid beside me on the bed.

"Feel better?" he asked.

"How did you know I needed that when I didn't even know it myself?"

"I know things." He smirked.

I was about to say something sarcastic when his hand ran down my thigh and up to my stomach before lingering just under the edge of my underwear.

"Now make the other phone calls you need to, let me be right again, and then I'll reward you in my own special way."

"You don't play fair."

"Never have. Never will."

After leaving me with a kiss on the lips, Alex bounced off the bed and began to saunter towards the door.

"Where are you going?" I called out to him suddenly.

With his fingers gripping the door handle, he looked back and smiled. "Baby, you don't need me here when you speak to Marcus and Sammy. This is something you have to do by yourself."

"Where are you going?" I repeated gently.

"You know where I'm going." And with that, he pulled open the door and walked out into the corridor, leaving me on the bed with my heart hammering in my chest.

I did know where he was going. I knew who he was about to call, and I knew the possible repercussions of him speaking to his father after leaving his bedside to join this journey with me.

I was nervous.

Nervous for what Nicholas might say to Alex. Nervous for what Sammy might say to me. Nervous about hearing any hint of sadness in Marcus's voice and my guilt eating me alive.

My hands shook as I pushed my laptop aside, picked up my phone and scrolled for Sammy's number. It took several rings for her to answer, and I swear those rings grew louder and more aggressive with each one that passed.

When I heard her voice and the reminder of how much I'd missed having my best friend in my life every day hit me, I clasped a hand over my mouth to catch a sob I could never have anticipated forming.

"Hello?" she repeated. "Nat, are you there? Is that you?"

I moved my hand away to speak, pushing my shoulders back as I tried to find the fortitude to be honest with the one person who'd always been honest with me.

"Sammy?" I croaked.

"Nat? What's wrong? What's happened? You sound…"

"Upset?"

"Yeah. Has something happened? Has Alex—"

"Nothing has happened. Alex is great. I'm great. I just miss you, Sammy."

Her silence lingered down the phone before she eventually let out a small, resigned sigh. "I miss you, too."

"Tell me the truth. Do you hate me for leaving your brother?"

"Nat," she breathed out. "We've been over this."

"We have, and I know you told me you were fine with it. I know you told me that you wanted me to be happy, but I can't shake this feeling that you're disappointed."

"What do you want me to say?" Her voice was soft and unsure. It was a voice of hers I didn't hear often.

"I want you to get all your frustrations out and let me know what you think of me."

"I don't want to do that."

"Why? Because you're scared of saying what you really think of me?"

"You don't get it, do you?" she snapped suddenly, a sardonic laugh falling from her. "I'm not mad at you, you silly cow. Jesus, Natalie! I've known it was Alex all along. Marcus has known it was Alex all along. Even your bloody parents have known it was Alex from the very first moment they saw the two of you together. If your dad interfering wasn't enough to let you know how everyone in your life was secretly rooting for you two then I don't know what else will. I'm happy for you. I love you very much. You're like a sister to me. I'm over the moon that you are with the man you belong with because deep down I always knew he was who you were destined to love."

"Then why have things seemed strange between us?"

"Because I should hate you, and I feel guilty as shit about that. My loyalty is totally torn in two. I should be on my brother's side. I should feel like you screwed him over… and I don't feel any of that because all I can think when I look at Marcus is *you dumb fucking idiot. I tried to warn you not to get too close to her. You brought this on yourself.*"

"I'm sorry I messed it up for all of us."

"Do me a favour. Quit saying sorry. Anyone who loves you doesn't need to hear it. We just want you to be happy. Marcus will be fine. He just needs space to figure out what he wants from his life. He's always needed someone to look after, and now he's wandering around like a damn dog that doesn't know how to find its lost puppy. Deep down he always knew this was going to happen. I just hope that one day you two can be good friends again. You were fun together."

I smiled at the thought, but it was a sad smile. Marcus and I had parted on good terms, but as the days had passed and the checking in to make sure everything was okay texts died down, I felt the chasm growing in our friendship.

"I don't know, Sam. It's a lot to ask of him no matter how much I'd love to have him back in my life."

I heard her shuffling on the other end of the phone, and from the noise in the background, I imagined her in some small coffee shop in the centre of Leeds, sitting by a window and watching the world pass her by.

"I love you, Nat. Sometimes friends need some breathing space as much as couples do, that's all."

I nodded, knowing she couldn't see me. "I just needed to hear your voice. I miss you."

"I miss you."

"Maybe when I get to Greece you can come out and see us."

"Us? Is Alex going to Greece with you, too?"

"He'd better be. I've spent long enough away from him."

"Ain't that the truth?"

I laughed quietly, dropping my bottom back down on the edge of the mattress while I stared out of my own window and took in the London skyline.

"So, tell me," she began. "On a scale of one to ten, just how fucking good is Alex Law in the sack?"

My laughter bubbled. "He's a definite seven hundred."

"Seven hundred, huh? I knew it!"

"He's amazing, Sammy. In every way. Not just under the

covers. I feel like I'm me again. No. Wait. I feel like I'm me for the first time ever, actually."

"That makes me happier than you'll ever know. You want to know what else makes me happy?"

"Sure." I grinned.

"The fact that I can *finally* talk about sex with you again. There was no way I was going to ask you how my own brother flipped you around on a mattress, but now..." She sighed dreamily. "Get ready for some dirty, dirty questions. I've finally got my best friend back, and I intend to abuse my position of power to learn the mysteries of Alexander fucking Law."

SIX

Dragging in a deep breath, I found Marcus's name in my phone and hit the call button.

Five rings passed.

Soon it was more than ten.

"Hey, this is Marcus. If you're my girlfriend, you'll probably wonder who Marcus is, 'cause all you've ever known me as is Big Daddy. Hey, Nat. If this is my parents, that'll be weird. I know. Oh, and if you're calling about that thing, I swear to you, I didn't smoke weed in college. If this is my sister, no I don't have any money to lend you. You don't need a boob job, Sammy! Anyone else, please leave a message after the beep and hope that I like you enough to get back to you."

He hadn't changed his message since we'd split up. He probably hadn't even realised.

"Erm, hey, Marcus. It's… Natalie. I was just calling to check in. I don't know why. That's a lie. I do know why. We said we'd stay friends, and I know it's only been a matter of days, but the longer I don't hear from you, the more I start to worry that you might not want that anymore."

The sound of the key card in the door had my head shooting up. Alex walked back in with his sagging shoulders, tired eyes, and a look on his face that made my heart feel like it was in a vice.

"Call me if you need me for anything. Or text me—whichever you prefer. You're still one of the most important people in my life. I hope you know that. Take care, Marcus."

When I hung up, I tossed the phone on the bed and made my way over to Alex.

"You okay?" I asked quietly.

He gave a few weak nods, blew the air out of his cheeks and grimaced. Alex's eyes were narrowed, and that goddamn 'V' had formed over them again, transforming him back into the teenage boy who had too much weight on his shoulders and not enough muscle in his heart to carry it anymore.

"He's drunk. Again," Alex said calmly. "Nothing different from what I expected really."

"I'm sorry, Alex."

He closed the gap between us and wrapped his arms around my waist. "He is who he is. He's never going to change. He doesn't want to."

"Do you want to go home?"

"What for?" He scowled.

"To be with him. To make sure he doesn't end up in hospital again."

Alex huffed out a short laugh. "After what he's just said to me? Not a chance."

"What did he say?"

"It doesn't matter. But it makes it easier for me to walk away from him when he's like this. It makes it easier to try and live my own life. I can't make him change if he doesn't want to."

"I just don't want you to regret any time you spend with me," I said quietly.

"He's already stolen five precious years of my life with you. He's robbed me of twenty-two years of living for myself. There's no way I'm going to wake up at forty-five and wish I'd focused on my own happiness instead of trying to force him to remember he's even alive."

"I've asked Barbara to keep her eye out for him at the centre," I admitted a little sheepishly.

Alex smirked and raised a brow. "I have Cleveland watching out for him, too. Pippa has said she will step in and help if she can. Cleveland told me Barbara has already been treating Dad like he's a foster child she's taken on. *Where is he? When did you last see him? You need any extra help, doc, and you just let me know. I'll show him some tough love. The kind of tough love that knocks you to your knees and doesn't help you get back up.*"

"That sounds like my girl." I chuckled.

"Trust me, Nat. There's no place on Earth I want to be but right here with you."

Reaching for his biceps, I trailed my palms up and down his arms. I wasn't in any position to tell Alex how to deal with his dad. I wasn't in any position to tell anyone how to live their lives—not while I was still figuring out what to do with my own.

"As long as you're sure." I slid my arms around his neck and went up on tiptoes, so my lips were closer to his.

"I'm sure," he whispered, swaying me in his arms. "How did it go with Sammy?"

"You were right… again." His face brightened, but he didn't say anything. "She's just excited we can start talking about sex again. She couldn't ever ask me about the intimate details while I was with her brother."

Alex froze, his eyes widening. "Talking about sex, how?"

"Well, hmm, let's see. She asked me what kissing you was like."

"Amazing," he answered for me abruptly.

"Naturally. She asked me how much you were packing in the trouser department."

"No, she didn't."

"Oh, she did."

"You girls are vicious," he said through a feigned gasp.

"Don't worry. I was extremely complimentary. I think I even made her eyes water a little."

"Say more things like that." He grinned.

"She asked me if we'd, you know, *reconnected*."

"And you told her sex with me was phenomenal, right?"

"I said you were okay." I shrugged. His fingers reached down to pinch the top of my arse cheeks, and I yelped in surprise. "Fine. I may have said something along the lines of feeling like I was on another planet. I don't know. I guess *other-worldly* slipped out somewhere along the way." I rolled my eyes, unable to remove the goofy grin from my face.

"Other-worldly, huh? Like Mars?"

"Hmm. Too close. Farther than that."

"Jupiter?" He beamed.

"I was thinking more…"

"Please tell me you did not say Uranus."

I burst out laughing, dropping my head to his chest as my body shook in his arms and tears formed in my eyes. His own laughter made his chest bounce against me, and the low rumble of his happiness made me want to freeze-frame the very moment we were living in and never, ever leave it.

When we calmed down and he pulled my chin back up so he could see my face, I sighed in contentment.

"Look at us, living the dream," he said.

I opened my mouth to respond, but the sound of my phone buzzing on the bed had us both turning to look at it.

When I saw Marcus's name flashing on the screen, I felt my heart being torn in two all over again. I wasn't sure I could speak to him with Alex there.

"You should take that. Talk to him." I looked up at Alex, my expression blank. "I'd have wanted you to talk to me if your decision had been different. You need to look after him the way he looked after you when I wasn't around." He smiled flatly at me before he thumbed over his shoulder. "I'll go grab a shower. Take as long as you need."

Just like that, my future was gone, and I reached down to take a call from my past that I was, admittedly, scared to take.

"Marcus?" I answered carefully, not wanting to sound sad, happy or… anything.

"Natalie!" he shouted. The background noise was horrific, a heavy bass making the speakers strain to take in the sound, the crackling forcing me to cringe.

"Marcus?" I called out a little louder, sticking a finger in my other ear to try and hear him better. "Are you there?"

"I'm here. I'm here! It's a bit bloody loud, I know. Wait... can you hear me now?"

"Hardly. It's so noisy. Where are you? It's the middle of the day. Are you okay?"

"Are you shitting me, little Nat? I'm fanfuckingtastic!"

The sound of glasses knocking together around him had my brows pulling together even tighter. I could hear men's laughter followed by a few feminine giggles. "Look, if now isn't a good time, we can chat later," I offered, my stomach swirling with unease for a reason I couldn't quite put my finger on.

Marcus laughed. He laughed in a way I'd rarely heard him laugh while he was with me. It sounded free. Rough. A little manic.

"Are you frowning, Nat? You are, aren't you? You're wondering where I am—if I'm safe. You're probably lifting that thumb of yours to your mouth right about now so you can chew on a nail in worry."

I paused mid lift of my hand and stared at my thumb, which was now just a few centimetres away from my mouth before I lowered my arm and rolled my eyes.

"What happened to you going and finding your happily ever after? Not giving a shit about what anyone thinks or does anymore? Isn't this supposed to be your time away from worrying?"

I sank onto the edge of the mattress in our room as I struggled to find a good response to that. In the end, the only thing I could come up with was, "Yes."

"Then why are you on the phone with me acting twitchy? Why aren't you with Trevor?"

"*Alex*," I reminded him softly, feeling a weak smile tug at the corner of my mouth.

"Who?"

"You're an idiot," I told him, huffing out a humourless laugh. "You know his name is Alex."

"Oh, yeah. That's the guy. Why are you phoning me when you're meant to be with him?"

A girl in the background let out a shriek of laughter before he told someone somewhere to quieten down. It gave me time to realise that I had no reason to lie to this man anymore. I should never have lied to him to start with.

"I am with him. We're having the most amazing time. Things feel… I don't know…"

"… how they never quite felt with me."

I stared down at my legs to pick at something that wasn't even there. "I'm happy," I said quietly. "What about you?"

"I'm having fun. A lot of fun. Where it will lead to, I don't know, but I'm happy enough for now."

"You sure?"

"As sure as eggs are eggs."

My smile was weak, even though I felt a sudden rush of love for the man I was speaking to. A platonic love. A love for the guy who held me in the back of a cab when my heart broke in his lap. A love for a guy who occupied my mind, made me grow, made me a better person just by being around. A love for a guy I was determined to keep in my life as anything but a lover.

"Marcus, I need you to promise me one thing."

"What's that?"

"If, at any point, you feel like things aren't going okay, like you aren't quite where you want to be, you go home. You go to your parents or to Sammy. You don't drink away your life in some dark bar in the middle of the day pretending to laugh and smile for everybody else's sake."

"You got it, little Nat."

"That wasn't a promise."

"I promise."

"Thank you." I smiled softly. "Oh, and Marcus?"

"Yeah?"

"If you're going to go home with anyone today, avoid the girl in the background who shrieks like a cat. Mrs Hawkins in the apartment below you will flip her lid if that woman is keeping her awake with her howling all night long."

Marcus's laughter tore free. "Mrs Hawkins can kiss my lily white…"

SEVEN

Alex had been right about everything. I had needed to speak to Mum, Dad and Sammy. I'd also needed to speak to Marcus, despite me thinking that everything I'd had to say to him had already been said. But as I sat on the sofa opposite Alex, my feet resting on the coffee table between us as I watched him flickering through a magazine I'd never even heard of, I couldn't help but notice how relaxed he looked compared to me.

Resting my cheek on my fist, I let my head fall to one side while I playfully reached out my foot to tap against his ankle with the sole intention of disturbing him.

His hazel eyes flashed up at me, and that small smirk of his grew.

"I was just thinking…" I began.

Alex lowered his magazine, dropping it carefully to the couch before he got up to move around onto my sofa and sit down beside me. His eyes never wandered from mine, and I felt a tightening in my stomach when his hand slid over the top of my thigh, moving up and down slowly.

"Good thinking or bad thinking?"

"Tell me your secrets," I begged him in a breath.

"My secrets?" he asked, his brows pulling together in confusion.

"About the time we spent apart." I paused, choosing my next words carefully. "I know we said no more living in the past, but there's so much time we missed out on, and every time I find myself looking at you, this stampede of questions takes over my mind."

"What kind of questions?"

"I don't know." I shrugged lightly, trailing a finger down his cheek. "You're still the same Alex, but you're different, too."

"We both are," he countered quietly, "but who I was when I wasn't with you wasn't very nice. I don't even like to admit I was that guy."

"You were that bad?"

"Yeah… for a while. I regret how I blamed Mum. I regret how I added to her sadness. I hate the physical fights I got into with Dad. I hate the way I made Mum feel like she had to choose between the two of us. I'm full of battle scars that remind me of all that stuff, day in, day out. Every new morning is a fight for me. I have to push down the bad shit and focus on the good things—the future. Most of all, Nat, I just hate diving into those memories of my life without you in it. Imagining you with Marcus, knowing that he was good for you, and he was helping mend what I broke…" He trailed off and shook his head while his hand drifted farther up my thigh until he'd shifted me onto my side and pulled me closer, wrapping both his arms around my waist.

"Do you know what your problem is? You don't believe how good you are."

"What do you mean?"

"I mean…" I started, moving my hands up to the sides of his copper hair and running my fingers through the depths of it. "You only see the bad things you've done in your past. Not the good things you did. I was fifteen and sad. I was just a girl at the back of a crowd, and you were the one person who really saw me without even knowing my name."

"Well, that's because you were so damn gorgeous."

I rolled my eyes and smiled, ignoring his deflections. "Then I was sixteen, and I was still sad, but a little hopeful because of you. You didn't need to look out for me. You didn't need to smile at me on that bus, but you did it anyway."

"That was a selfish move on my part."

"No, it was because you cared."

Alex's eyes searched mine.

"Then I was seventeen, and I was in love with a boy. I was living again, feeling something after feeling nothing except like I'd died right along with my sister."

"Natalie," he whispered.

I smiled back at him. "And, even though this boy—this amazing, kind, and ridiculously handsome boy had troubles of his own—he took it upon himself to try to protect me from any more pain in life. He took a few emotional bullets because he thought he was saving me. So, maybe this was just the journey we were always meant to make. It all seems worth it because I'm here with you now… and you're looking at me like that." I grinned, noticing the way his eyes had darkened and his arms became tenser before he wrapped himself around me. He swept my legs underneath him and laid me back on the sofa until his whole body was towering over mine.

There's something special about the face a man makes when he's above you, devouring you with his eyes. He felt open and exposed to me whenever he was like this.

"Let's go someplace we haven't been yet. Let's do something we've never done before. Let's be young, carefree, and reckless. Let's get sweaty in a dark club somewhere. Let's drink, dance and lose ourselves in each other. Let's go wild together, Natalie Vincent."

"You're so cute." My grin was in danger of shattering my cheeks as my happiness shook my world and tipped it upside down.

"I'm sick of being cute. I want to show you the sides of me that not even I've discovered yet." Dropping his head, he brushed his lips over mine. "We've done the tragic teenage love thing. Tonight, I don't want us to be anything other than intensely R-rated. I want your whole body to burn for us and the future I know I can give you."

***

Alex made love to me on that sofa. It was the slow, sensual kind of lovemaking, where every movement is strong and fluid, where every breath is held tight in your chest until your head feels dizzy and you have to force yourself to breathe again.

It was perfect—so perfect that when he brought me back to life with several small kisses and ordered me to go shower and change, I did so on shaky legs and with a frantically dancing heartbeat.

My hair was done within thirty minutes, as was my make-up. When I stepped out of the bathroom, cosmetically ready but wearing nothing but a towel around me, I walked straight into

Alex's chest with a thump and stumbled backwards.

He, as always, had the most ridiculous display of arm porn waiting for me. It was my weakness. Everything about him made me melt, it was true, but his hands and arms? Those things had so many powers of their own. I knew what they could do to me with just one touch, but it was unbelievable what they could do to me by doing nothing at all. The muscles in them were perfectly defined, straining against the short sleeves of his black polo T-shirt, while the forearms were hidden behind his back, his hands clasped together.

Alex's small cough pulled my attention back to his face.

"You look beautiful." He smiled, looking sheepish.

I glanced down at my white towel and gave him a small twirl. "Thanks. I designed this myself."

"I was talking about your face, but you totally pull off the hotel chic look." He sucked in a deep breath, holding it in his chest before he released it and stepped forward, pulling his arms out in front of him to reveal a brown paper bag. "But, the other day, I saw something in the shop window of the boutique two doors down from here, and I kinda had to get it for you."

I reached for the bag and began to open it, my eyes wide as I pulled out the beautifully lined, black, lacy material that was inside. The paper bag eventually dropped to the floor while I held the dress out in front of me.

"You don't have to wear it," he began. "There was just something about it when I saw it, and I couldn't stop thinking about it being wrapped around you."

It was halter-neck—a style I didn't wear a lot, but something I knew would work as a good contrast against the length of my long blonde hair. It felt so thick, so rich, and when I spun it around in my hands, I saw that it was completely backless.

My eyes drifted up to meet Alex's just as he pushed both his hands into the front pockets of his grey trousers, tensing his arms even harder as he rocked back on the heels of his feet and bit down on his lip.

"Remember at Paul and Suzie's wedding when you wore that purple, open-backed dress?"

"I do," I whispered.

"Don't get mad if I keep touching you up all night, okay? I resisted you once back then when you were showing me that amazing body of yours, but now…"

I moved quickly, curling a hand around the back of his neck and pulling him down closer to me. "Now you don't have to hold back." Kissing him firmly, I eventually pulled away, loosened the towel from my chest, and let it fall to the floor. I climbed into the dress as carefully as I could before turning around and letting Alex fasten the necktie for me as I ran my hands over the amazing material that flowed out from the waist, resting just above my knees with a kiss of the fabric.

I heard him blow the air out of his cheeks when I broke away from him and spun around several times. I brushed my hands down the curves of my waist.

"What do you think?"

"I think…" He breathed out again, running a hand through one side of his hair as he studied the dress. "I think… I'm about to have a heart attack. Death by desire. But fuck, I can't think of a better way to go."

EIGHT

I saw the women looking at Alex when we walked into the first bar of the night, and I had to force myself to push down the small stirrings of jealousy that rumbled in my stomach.

With his arm wrapped around my waist, Alex guided me into the back of the Gem Bar in Soho, manoeuvring me effortlessly through the crowds that had already formed. There was never a quiet night in London—that was something we'd learned from our very first day there. City life was the epitome of hectic, lively, and awake. If you wanted to feel the beat of the world beneath your feet, all you had to do was step onto the streets and wait for it to flow right through you.

"Why were you so insistent on this place?" I asked him as he walked me forward, the palm of his hand moving to the exposed small of my back.

Alex ignored me, continuing to look straight ahead as if seeking something out.

"Alex?"

"Did you put any underwear on before we left that hotel room?"

"Nope."

"Oh, shit." He coughed to clear his throat, and I felt the press of his thumb against my skin. "I shouldn't have asked that question."

"What's wrong?" I asked through a satisfied giggle.

He stopped to look down at me before pointing towards the back of the bar. "We have visitors."

I pushed up onto tiptoes to try and see above the crowd. "Visitors? Who?"

"They've been nagging me to come down and see us both. Constantly nagging me, Nat. I've been brushing them off, but then I lay awake last night, and I realised that it was stupid. Even though we're spending this time alone together and, believe me, I fucking love it, all I've ever wanted to do is walk towards our friends with your hand in mine, feeling no shame, just pride that you're finally mine."

"Suzie and Paul?" I dared myself to ask, completely surprised by how utterly excited I was to see the two people who had been instrumental in making me see that Alex was who I was meant to be with.

"Is that okay?"

My cheeks flushed red before I closed the gap and pressed my mouth against his. I dragged out the kiss, pulling him forward and making him lose his balance until he had to grip the tops of my arms to steady himself. When I pulled away, I bit down on my bottom lip to taste him there, running my tongue over it slowly and seductively.

Glancing around, Alex discreetly dropped his hand to his trousers and rearranged himself as subtly as he could. His eyes closed and he swallowed heavily. "Please stop turning me on in front of Paul."

He grabbed my hand and began to walk us across the club. When I saw our two friends sitting around a small table filled with candles, I felt a rush of giddiness drop into the soles of my feet, forcing me to practically sprint forward. I must have squealed or done something very un-me-like because Suzie's head turned in my direction and before I could prepare myself, she was rushing towards me, screaming out my name before she flung her arms around my neck and rocked me in a vice-like grip.

"Natalie!"

"Suzie," I said through a huge grin.

"Oh, God, you're here, and I'm here, and…" She squeezed me harder. I felt like I was going to burst with happiness before she pulled away from me and held me at arm's length, her eyes drifting down my body slowly before rising back up to my face. "You look amazing."

"So do you."

"Nuh-huh. Not like you. I've never seen you look…" Her voice trailed off before she turned to look at Alex slowly. He was standing right beside me, shaking Paul's hand. "Happy," she finished.

"It's Alex. He brings out the best in me."

"I'm so proud of you."

"What for?"

"For finally doing what is right for you."

I offered her a smile before pulling her into another embrace. It didn't last long, though. Paul soon stepped around Alex and picked me up in his arms to spin me around.

As much as I wanted to laugh and hold him tight, I was also very aware of the fact that there wasn't anything underneath my dress to keep my decency intact. As if sensing my worry in an instant, Alex stepped forward and grabbed hold of Paul's shoulder to stop him from lifting me higher.

"Easy, Paul. That's my girl you've got your hands all over," he joked, while his free hand discreetly pushed the material of my dress down under the cheeks of my bum.

"Yeah, Paul. I'm taken." I laughed, peeling off him until my feet safely met the floor.

Paul glanced between the two of us with an incredulous look on his face. "Are you fucking shitting me? I've always been allowed to fool around with Nat."

"That's when she wasn't with me." Alex smirked.

"You're Nat-blocking me?"

"Damn right I am."

"Not even a butt grab?"

"Not even a nipple tweak."

"Well, fuck," Paul sighed. "Shit's changing too much lately."

"Oh, give up with yourself, Harris," Suzie scolded him, her eyes rolling to the ceiling as she shook her head. "Need I remind you that you're married now?" She lifted her wedding band up into his face and wiggled her finger.

"No, wifey. No reminder needed. You're the only woman that I want." He leaned forward, taking her finger between his teeth, causing a giggle of excitement to escape her.

Alex's hand slid along the base of my back before it settled on my waist and he pulled me closer to him. I held on to him tightly, wrapping my arms around him and resting my head on his chest as we watched Suzie and Paul's effortless banter. They complimented each other in ways that made it impossible to imagine either of them having a life before they were together.

Just like I found it hard to imagine how I survived before I knew Alex existed.

Still pressed against him, I looked up at his face at the same time as he glanced down at me, and when our smiles met, so many unspoken words were exchanged.

"Wow," Suzie said, forcing us to turn our attention back to her. Paul was standing behind her, his arms wrapped around her waist as they both studied us openly. "I'm sorry," Suzie croaked, getting emotional. "But I always hoped to see the two of you together like this. Don't get me wrong, I liked Marcus."

"Suzie," Paul warned, swaying her from side to side.

"No, no. Let me finish. I know I said Marcus' name, but it's not like he's *Voldemort*, right?"

Alex laughed freely. "Marcus is a good man."

"Exactly. We know that. There are no toes to step on here. No more eggshells to walk on. You two are out in the open now and you both know everything about each other's pasts, so we can say names and mention people."

"Bet Nat doesn't know *all* the names of Alex's past." Paul chuckled quietly in Suzie's ear, and I was aware that I probably wasn't meant to hear that. I couldn't help the frown that formed, and I didn't miss the way Alex had tensed around me before he exhaled a long and heavy breath.

Suzie either didn't hear her husband or she simply chose to ignore him. Her hands came up in front of her as her fingers created a frame for her to look through—one that would let her take a mental snapshot of me in Alex's arms. "But no matter what you both did while you were apart, here is where I always knew you'd end up."

"You look good together," Paul told us proudly.

Alex ran his free hand down over his mouth, giving me one final squeeze of attention before he reached out to Paul and shook his hand. "Cheers, mate. I probably wouldn't have gone back to Calverley if it hadn't been for you. Thanks for waking me up."

Something else I didn't know.

"What did Paul do?" I whispered as I looked back at Alex.

He smiled down on me, but I saw the sadness in his eyes before he dropped a kiss to my nose. "I'll tell you some other time. Let me get you a drink."

"Did I just hear the word drink?" Paul chimed in.

"Sure did. Let's get to the bar and leave these two ladies to catch up."

After a few more exchanges and a parting kiss from Alex, I watched them walk away together—two friends with more of a bond than I'd realised, and a man named Paul who could probably give me every answer to every question I'd ever had about my boyfriend.

All I had to do was figure out a way to make him tell me.

Was I really that desperate to dig?

Shouldn't I just enjoy the here and now, move forward and live out our happily ever after, the way Alex wanted me to?

I knew what my answers should have been, but I also knew I'd shoved too many things to the back of my mind too many times before. I'd done too much pretending and landed myself in too many dark holes of regret to last me a lifetime.

Who else had kissed Alex's lips? What had he been through with his father? How did he cope with the death of his mother? Did he have anyone looking after him the way he looked after me when Lizzy passed away?

If we were going to move forward—if we were going to enjoy this new time together, I had a feeling we were going to have to go backwards first. There were things—and I wasn't sure what or how important those things were—that Alex was keeping from me. Things that made my gut twist with an emotion I couldn't quite place. Things I knew I wasn't going to like, but things I knew I had to face, one way or another. I couldn't build a future on lies ever again. I wouldn't. Not with him.

NINE

We spent hours sitting around in that dimly lit bar, catching up on each other's lives. No matter how lost I got in the conversation, Alex's touch on my thigh, cheek, or exposed back never failed to make my skin flare to life with goosebumps.

"Look at you two, all cute and loved up. Not giving a single care in the world to ask us about our big day or even demanding to see more pictures of our wedding on the beach yet," Suzie grumbled with a smile on her face. "Anyone would think you'd been preoccupied."

My eyes lit up instantly, and Alex leaned farther over the table. "Are you kidding me?" he cried. "I asked Paul for pictures fucking weeks ago."

"You photo-blocked them?" Suzie's mouth hung limply before she turned to her husband.

"Nope," Paul croaked, half swallowing his drink while trying to get his words out. "I photo-blocked *him*." He pointed at Alex. "Let's not forget that when we got married, these two hadn't hooked back up yet. He was still the depressed, brooding man with a broken heart and a chip on his shoulder the size of a fucking beast."

My legs tensed beneath the table, and my hand slid over Alex's thigh. "Well, he isn't depressed, brooding, or living with a broken heart now, you guys, so we'd both really like to see them. In fact," I eyed Alex carefully with a smirk on my face, "we're a little bit hurt you two didn't want us, your supposed best friends, there for your big day. You know… the real one."

"Oh," Paul gasped, his mouth exaggerating his expression as he clasped his hands to his cheeks. "See, Suzie, I always told you there was a demon behind that angelic smile of hers. So manipulative." Paul dropped his hands on the table and laughed. "Natalie Vincent, I do believe you just tried to make us feel guilty without just cause."

"Guilty as charged. What can I say? I get protective of my man."

Alex leaned back, and his arm fell around my shoulders before he tilted his head to one side and raised a brow at Paul. "Her man. Did you hear that, Harris?"

"I heard it and I choked on its sickly sweetness." He grinned, picking up his drink and knocking the remainder of his beer back in one gulp. When his glass landed back on the table, he reached over for his phone and began to scroll through. "Here, you whiny, love-struck puppies. Have a gander at what true love looks like."

I reached over to take the phone in my hand while Alex peered at it from beside me. The first thing that struck me was the vibrant colours that surrounded them both. Bright blue skies, aqua oceans, and sand so white it was almost blinding. Yet, in the middle of all that stood two young people in love.

Two people who nobody would have expected to have their shit together as much as they did. Paul and Suzie were always meant to be just a fling, yet here I was, looking down on imagery so perfect it was almost book cover worthy. Their eyes were alive as they gazed at one another and said their vows. As I flicked through the photos, I fell more and more in love with what I was seeing between them—a spark that was invisible yet was so apparent we all should have been able to touch it.

"It was the single best day of my life." Suzie sighed.

"Mine, too, babe," Paul agreed.

"It's like something from a movie," I told them. "You're incredible together. You always have been."

Suzie reached over for the phone, holding it between us to direct me to another picture. When she got to it, a photo album stared back at me—one that was as thick as *War and Peace*—and on the front cover was a picture of Paul and Suzie aged fifteen. Two young, wild-looking kids who, even back then, were gazing adoringly into one another's eyes.

"This album was a gift from my parents. I had no idea how they got all those memories, but apparently, Sammy and Danni had a lot to do with collating the photos, and Paul and I had always been generous with the pictures we shared on Facebook," she admitted with a small laugh. "But do you see that picture on the front, Nat? That's my favourite one. If I could go back to that girl and tell her everything would work out, that we'd definitely end up together, I would do it in a heartbeat. I'd tell her not to over-analyse the little things, and to trust that when two people love each other, there is no way they'll ever be apart. Not even raging hormones and high school dramas."

"I wish I had pictures together from when Alex and I were teenagers," I found myself saying without thought. "It would be nice to have memories to look back on—to see how we were with each other. I guess my years of pretending allowed me to forget about silly things like that."

Alex coughed beside me, suddenly fidgety as he cast his eyes down into his lap before looking back up at Paul.

Paul smirked, quickly dipping his head and shaking it in some kind of disbelief.

"Sorry," I mumbled. "I didn't mean to say that out loud."

"Shit, she really does have no idea, does she?" Paul whispered into Suzie's ear as he pressed himself against her. Another thing I was sure I wasn't meant to hear, but I guess Paul wasn't as discreet as he thought.

"Paul," Alex warned.

Suzie sighed heavily and shook her head as she glanced down at the table.

"What?" I asked them, but not one of them looked at me, and I was quickly growing tired of being the only one who wasn't in on the jokes. Exhaling, I peeled myself away from Alex and rested both my arms on the table in front of me. I didn't want to ruin this night with our friends, but I couldn't deny feeling like the one kid at the party who wasn't wearing the right costume.

"Natalie," Alex breathed beside me, his arms trying to curl around my waist.

I pushed him off as carefully as I could and stared at Paul, unjustifiably putting my irritation on him.

I took a moment to make sure my voice was calm, even and reasonable. "Paul, you and Suzie didn't screw up the way we did. I know that. You secured your happily ever after in the school corridors while I watched mine push through those doors and walk away. I've spent five years pretending, secretly wishing I could know what he's been doing and what I'm missing out on. I've spent so long ashamed of myself, filled with guilt and anger for not being able to be with him." I turned to look at Alex, hoping he could see the slight hurt in my eyes. "Now that I have you, please don't make me feel out of the loop by casting those little looks at each other. I know there are things private to you guys, and I have no right to feel left out of a time when I wasn't present in your life… but I wanted to be there. So, whatever has made you pull that awkward-looking face from me saying I wanted memories with you, just tell me. Please. I can handle it. Even if your secrets will hurt me."

"Hurt you? What? Why do you always assume the worst?"

"I don't. I…"

"Yes, you do."

"He's right, you do," Paul agreed.

"I third that accusation," Suzie muttered quietly.

"I do?"

"Babe, I get that you suffered because of me. I get that you hated the time we spent apart almost as much I did. I get that you're waiting for something to go wrong, even when you think you're living for the moment. I get that this might take some adjusting to. But do not, for one minute, ever think that I am laughing at *you*. My shame, my blame, and my embarrassment lands at *my* feet. Paul's a dick who takes every opportunity he gets to laugh at me, not with me. It's never about you."

"Wow. He's right again. I've never agreed with him twice in one night," Paul stated with mock surprise.

I ignored him, keeping my eyes on Alex. He looked determined as he pulled his phone out of his pocket and dropped it unceremoniously on the table in front of me.

Waving a hand over it like he didn't have a care in the world, Alex raised both brows and smiled flatly. "You want to know what

Paul is talking about? Not a problem. Just have a scroll through the album entitled Natalie and see for yourself how much I missed you before I even let you go."

The breath I held high in my chest ached to be released, but I couldn't seem to grant myself the relief until I hit the button and saw the first picture of me, aged sixteen, lying on my back in the overgrown grass of the park, my arms in the air, staring up at the bright blue skies above me.

I stared at the young girl I barely recognised.

It was just one picture—a simple moment in time—yet as I stared at the me from six years earlier, all I could think about was how I wanted to do what Suzie had just told me. There was a need to go back to young Natalie and warn her of her impending heartbreak. There was a need to go to her and cradle her in my, now stronger, arms. A craving to protect her, but to also tell her that the pain would be worth it the moment Alex found her again just a few years later.

My eyes flickered to Alex with embarrassment, and I saw his own awkwardness glaring back at me.

"Keep going," he whispered.

I did as I was instructed, returning my attention to the phone and scrolling through.

So many images were there, various moments in time where I hadn't been looking at the camera on his phone, or even been aware of the fact he was considering taking a photo of me. There were several of me lying on his chest in bed, snapshots of my hand in his, my fingers tracing his T-shirt, or our legs entwined. The pictures were never full images of my face or of us smiling. It seemed Alex had taken little mental snapshots to remember me by, focusing on the smaller details of us together that I would never have thought to capture. My heart was about to burst as I continued to scroll through. There were hundreds. Some powerful enough to make me gasp quietly to myself, and some I couldn't work out the significance of. But they must have meant something to him.

The sun shone down on my hands as I made a daisy chain in the park with him, my legs crossed, and my eyes focused on my work as he snapped away without me realising. Then there were pictures of me standing in the school playground with my folders pressed to my chest, pictures of me laughing freely while standing amongst my girlfriends, my head tilted back, and my eyes closed as I enjoyed some fleeting feeling of guilt-free happiness.

When I found the last set of pictures in the album, I almost stopped breathing altogether. It summed up the beginning of our relationship perfectly. It probably wouldn't look like much to anyone else, but I knew the significance of those last images. We were on the bus, and Alex was sitting behind me, taking pictures of the back of my head, my hair changing colour as the seasons changed through the photos. Pictures of me wearing woolly hats in the winter versus my hair up in a ponytail as the sun kissed it through the window, the light hitting my crown enough to make it seem like I had a damn halo above my head.

He'd captured so much.

I was speechless.

I was overwhelmed.

I had never loved him more than I did right then.

More than anything, it reaffirmed to me how much he'd always loved me.

Placing the phone back down on the table, I stared down at my lap and allowed myself a moment to collect some composure. Despite the music in the bar, there was an eerie calm around our table. I knew everyone's eyes were fixed firmly on me, waiting for my reaction, and suddenly the thought of how much love I had for Alexander Law no longer allowed me to stop my small smile from breaking free.

I peeked up at him through my lashes.

His eyes narrowed as he shuffled in his seat, and when he raised his brows and cleared his throat, I launched my attack. Pushing myself up, I wrapped my arms around his neck fiercely, crashing my lips against his with enough force to knock him off balance and send us both falling back into the booth where we sat. His strong arms wasted no time in holding on to me, somehow smoothing down the edges of my dress to keep my modesty intact before wrapping themselves around my waist with a possession I prayed would always make me tingle this way.

"Eww, for fuck's sake," Paul grumbled.

"I think it's amazing," Suzie cried. "I feel like I'm watching some kind of romantic stage show play out right before my eyes."

"More like a horror," Paul muttered.

I didn't need to see it to know Suzie had just slapped him somewhere, probably up the back of the head again. His *ouch* of surprise followed by his own assault on her had them both squealing like two equally lovesick puppies, but I didn't allow myself to focus on them for long.

Opening my eyes, I looked down at Alex. My hands found both sides of his head and my fingers pushed themselves through the thicker parts of his hair. "I am so in love with you."

"Say that to me again." Rotating his hips beneath me, Alex let his hands slide over the tops of my arse cheeks, his smile beyond seductive as he inhaled slowly. "Say you're in love with me."

"I am head over heels... in love... with you."

His groan rumbled deep in the back of his throat, and his eyes darkened in a way that would have had me in a lot of good trouble had we been back in our hotel room.

"The things you do to me, Natalie Vincent. The things you do."

TEN

"**T**his bar here. Look. It's karaoke," Paul proclaimed as we walked through the streets of London, looking for someplace else to go that was a bit livelier than the seductive, highbrow ambience of the bar we'd just been in.

"You a good singer, Paul?" I asked with a smile on my face.

"There isn't anything I'm not good at." He winked.

"Except modesty," Suzie grumbled beside him.

"Who needs modesty these days? Everyone is so self-deprecating. It's good for one of us to own up to being cool as fuck."

Alex's arm tightened around me as he barked out a laugh and shook his head. "Big words for you there, Harris. You swallowed a dictionary?"

"Hey! I don't swallow anything that starts with dic… you hear me?"

"Yet he expects me to every night." Suzie chuckled.

"Are we going in or not?" Alex asked, taking charge.

"Crap it. I forgot how good you could sing. You're desperate to show me up, ain't you, Alex?" Paul hit back.

"A bit of competition is healthy."

"Only because you know you're going to win this one."

"Maybe." Alex grinned.

I raised my chin and angled my face to look up at the man in my arms. He was a good singer? How and why didn't I know this?

"You can sing?" I asked.

"I can hold my own."

Paul glanced at me, and when I caught his eyes, I knew he'd read my look of surprise.

Turning back to Alex, he gestured to me with his thumb. "Have you two actually done any talking since you got back together?"

"We've been busy." Alex laughed.

"I can tell. Does she know you play piano, too?"

"You play piano?" I gasped.

Alex scratched the back of his neck, obviously a little embarrassed. "Not very well, but I've had a dabble over the years."

"I didn't know."

"Only because I haven't had the chance to tell you yet."

"I didn't know you could sing, either."

His eyes narrowed as he studied my face and I knew I couldn't hide that tiny bit of hurt I felt from him. "Natalie?"

"Yeah?"

"Don't go there," he said quietly, leaning forward until he was close enough to allow his breath to wash over me.

"It's weird finding things out about you from someone else. It's been a night full of surprises for me already."

Stroking my cheek with a single finger, he stared at me and let his eyes search mine intently. He could see what I was thinking. I'd never been good at lying to him, of all people.

"I'm sure there are things about you that I don't know, but we have all the time in the world to figure it out. Rome wasn't built in a day. What we have is going to be amazing, but we have to take it one moment at a time. I'm not hiding anything. I just haven't stopped screwing you enough yet to take the time to talk about five years' worth of history. I can always put you on a sex ban if that's what you'd prefer?" His eyes were challenging, and his jaw ticked as he struggled to contain his swoon-worthy smile.

"Fine, Mr. I-Play-Piano-I-Sing-I-Take-Secret-Pictures-I'm-So-Full-Of-Surprises. I'll be patient," I conceded. "Just… quit being so perfect, okay? You're making it hard for me to keep up with you."

"Still, after all these years, you don't see yourself clearly at all."

***

It was true—Alex could sing. He had these rough, gravelly, low tones that sucked you in and made you feel like he was spreading his voice all over your skin, giving you his very own concert with his tongue.

I had never been more turned on than I was watching him up on that stage with Paul. They sang a collection of songs, some of which I'd heard of and some of which I hadn't, but no matter what he was delivering to the crowd, my stomach tightened with want.

"Pretty dreamy, isn't he?" Suzie said, nudging me out of my daze as her glass clinked against mine on the table.

I forced myself to tear my eyes away from the small stage where they were currently in fits of laughter after Paul had tried, and failed epically, to hit the high note of Whitney Houston's, *I Will Always Love You*—a song he was singing for Suzie with the help of Alex as his backing vocalist.

"Paul?" I asked.

"*No,*" she said with a laugh. "Paul's a fucking idiot. I was talking about your man. The man who seems to have it all."

I sighed in agreement, resting my chin on my fist as I stared at her and just fluttered my eyelashes.

"He seems to have everything—especially the girl who can't believe her own luck."

"I can't," I answered honestly, my brows rising. "Have you seen him? Would any woman think they deserved him?"

"Doesn't matter what any woman thinks, though, does it? Only you. He could be with that Rosie-Huntingdon-Big-Luscious-Lips woman every guy out there wants, but he'd still be thinking of you. He's fucking besotted."

"I know. I just…"

Her hand covered mine. "You're just waiting for your next bubble to burst."

"Stupid, isn't it?"

"Not even a little bit. It's hard to know how to be real when all you've known is how to pretend. It isn't just a switch you can flick. It isn't just something you can change. I've been with you for just a few hours tonight, and every time you smile I see a flicker of fear flash over your face. It's like you're scared of being happy."

"Christ. You and Sammy should have been in the secret service together or something. You see too much."

"So I'm right?" She smiled sadly.

"I don't know, Suze. I have this tiny little nagging voice in the back of my head that's warning me to be careful. It's like I'm confused, and I don't *want* to be confused anymore. I want to move forward, but yeah, there's a small part of me that's sad we didn't have this sooner. If he decided to leave me again…" My brows pulled together. "I'm not saying he will. I know he loves me, and he's different now. He's not afraid to show me what he really feels. I just don't know how I would even begin to deal with it if he did leave, and I don't ever want this happiness to stop. I didn't expect my fairy tale ending would have me stumbling into another irrational problem."

"There are no problems, only worries. Two totally different things. What you're feeling is normal. It's a risk we take when we go after what we really want. You don't think that I worry about Paul's outlandish flirting with every girl he meets? Of course I do, but I choose to rise above it because I trust him. There's always a fear that someone might catch his eye more than I do, but I can't run the risk of pushing him away based on a bunch of maybes. And anyway, whatever happens, it's better to have loved and lost and all that jazz, right?" She chuckled, right when I was expecting her to do anything but laugh. "You and I are different, though. I know that. I know what kind of girl you are. You're the kind who feels everything deeply now after so many years of feeling nothing. The gates have been opened. You feel guilty all the damn time. You still feel guilty for living when your sister, who seemed to have life so figured out, isn't."

"Fuck," I whispered, acknowledging the sting of that truth right in my gut like a knife had just been pushed into me.

"Sometimes friends have to be the ones to say the things you don't want to tell yourself." Suzie's fingers tightened over mine. "You are someone so beautiful of heart, you hate the thought of others suffering so you've decided to go on a one-woman crusade to save every bit of suffering for yourself. You're damaged, yet pure, and my God, you are the most beautiful soul that I have ever had the honour of calling my friend."

I refused to cry, although I supposed my tears would be of happiness and good fortune at that moment. I was rich in ways that money didn't even enter into.

"You're allowed to have doubts. Just don't let them steal your joy."

Alex's voice over the microphone dragged my attention back to him, and when I looked up, our eyes met across the room. His smile was intoxicating, and his body was strong. His eyes were alive with happiness for the entire world to see. But his heart… that was mine only, and didn't that make me the luckiest being alive?

Hoping he couldn't see even a hint of my worry, I pushed my lips together to blow him a kiss, and like the openly in love man that he was, he pretended to catch it before pushing it into his chest and winking back at me.

"See?" Suzie cried. "That fool is so in love with you. It's like I can feel it flowing around the room trying to choke me."

"All right, all right," I said, laughing and running my hands over my cheeks in embarrassment. "I get it. You've made your point. Now get me another drink, and stop being so bloody wise and grown up."

Lifting her glass to her mouth, she drained her drink and smacked her lips together. "What can I say? Married life has made me like some kind of prophet. I lead the donkeys to the water and let them drink I'm the kind of person who keeps this world going."

"And married life has clearly made you as modest as your husband."

We laughed, and it wasn't long until the guys came over to join us, sliding into their seats before they argued over the songbook that sat proudly on the table.

They argued over who would sing what song next, while Suzie and I sat back like mothers of children who had to be left to settle their own fallouts for themselves.

"If you try and sing Bee Gees, you will clear this place out," Alex told Paul.

"Screw you. Just because I didn't spend the last five years in my room sulking and singing that depressing-as-shit song, it doesn't make me a bad singer."

"Shut it," Alex barked back through a laugh.

"Wait. What *was* that song you always had on whenever we spoke on the phone?" Paul pushed.

Alex ran his hand up the back of his neck, his brows rising high as he stared at the table and shrugged. "Dunno, mate. I listened to a lot of music. Let's just pick something from the book already."

"No," Paul said, gasping after taking a quick sip of his beer. "You know which one I'm talking about, don't you?"

"Not a clue," he ground out.

Paul pointed at him, clicking his fingers as he tried to hum the tune as it slowly came back to him. "It went like this," he went on, and after just a few seconds more, I recognised the song.

"Isn't that—?" I started, only to be cut off by Suzie.

"It's *Creep* by Radiohead!" she shouted out, as if she were calling *Bingo!*

"That's it." Paul grabbed Suzie's cheeks, pulling her in for a kiss. "You're so clever, wifey." He turned back to Alex, settling himself closer to Suzie who was now wearing a proud look of satisfaction on her face. "You always had that shit on in the background."

"Careful who you're calling shit, Harris. Radiohead are the bollocks."

"I never understood the deal with that tune.It always seemed fucking morbid to me."

"I guess I just connected with it."

I knew that song. I knew it well. I had my own interpretation of it, and from the body language Alex was giving off, I guessed that he had, too. My hand slid over the top of his, pulling his attention back to me.

"I love that song," I told him.

"So do I±—or did. Now it just reminds me of a time I'd rather forget."

"Why?"

He pressed his lips tight, rubbing them together. "Maybe if I sang it, you'd understand a little better."

"I'm all ears," I offered with a reassuring smile.

It didn't take him long to get back up on the stage again, but there was no denying that this time, Alex looked nervous. His body was stiff, his shoulders tight as he made his way to the spotlight just a few minutes later. He'd already become a firm favourite with the audience, so it was no surprise to me when he was welcomed with loud cheers and squeals from the more outlandish women at the front of the small crowd.

I couldn't hide my pride. He looked beautiful up there. He deserved every ounce of attention.

Alex lifted a hand to the women in thanks, smiling flatly before he shuffled around on his feet and spun the microphone in his palm once. I could feel his nerves from over here, and it made the hairs on the back of my neck stand to attention.

"Okay," he started, making no attempt to hide the subtle clearing of his throat before he rubbed his hand up the back of his neck again. "I'm going solo for this one, guys. Don't hate on me if I screw this up or if it sends you to sleep."

The cheers grew louder, and I had to wonder if he had any

idea how much he had the crowd in the palms of his hands, or if he had any idea how he held the whole damn world there.

"This is for my girl. The one who *almost* got away."

His eyes met mine through the harsh lights of the bar.

Then it started, and I had no idea how something so tragic, how words so hypnotic—laced with pain and doubt yet somehow tinged with a tiny bit of hope—could break me apart and put me back together again. He was right; it did remind me of a worse time. But he was wrong about me almost getting away.

He was so fucking special.

I'd have always found my way back to him eventually.

ELEVEN

Not long after, we left the karaoke bar and headed to a nightclub.

I tried to remember every single detail I could, such as the flash of blue and green strobe lights that ran across Alex's face and lit up his eyes in the darkness. I tried to hold on to the way his muscles tensed around me while he guided me to somewhere safe, away from the riffraff of the night.

It wasn't easy living that way, though, and the more the night wore on, the more I realised that trying to enjoy the moment versus trying to pause and soak it in left my mind in total confusion, pulling one way one minute and another the next.

Hold it. Enjoy it. Freeze-frame. Live for now. Don't forget this. Let your mind go.

I needed two of me—one to feel and experience, the other to look over us both, make memories, take pictures, and write down every little thing that was happening with us.

Finally, I gave and relaxed, letting my spine fall against Alex's chest. We were high up on a balcony, looking down on the busy dance floor where Paul and Suzie were unashamedly putting on an X-rated version of *Dirty Dancing* without a care in the world.

Alex pushed me forward against the barrier, effectively wedging me in so I had nowhere to go, and the minute he pressed his hips against mine, I felt his arousal, causing my lazy smile to grow.

Our bodies began to move together, weaving a figure of eight—a perfect infinity sign with our hips, as I lifted my arm and reached around to grip the back of his neck, while my free hand clung onto the balcony ledge.

Alex didn't say anything, but I could feel his satisfied smile as he dropped his lips to my neck and began to nibble at my skin. God, he felt good. He smelt incredible, too. There had always been something about him, some calling to me that made me want to drown in the cloud of his scent. My stomach tightened at the thought and right on cue, his hand pushed down to press against it, his fingertips brushing so low on the lace material, it felt like he was touching every nerve ending that was alive down there.

I picked up the pace, rocking our bodies even harder together and digging my nails into the nape of his neck, teasing him with my arse cheeks. I didn't care who was around us or who was watching. All I cared about was feeling him. He was a man, so strong, so in control, and so confident when it came to showing me how his body could move. I wanted to show him how mine could do the same. I wasn't the woman he'd left behind, even though with him, I could have been a virgin, and I would still have known what to do because it was Alex I was responding to.

Nothing felt forced.

Nothing had to be thought about.

My need for him was primal, and it was raw.

"Alex…" I breathed out his name.

"Yeah, baby," he moaned beneath my ear, his tongue trailing up to my lobe where he pinched it between his teeth.

"I…"

With one hand on my stomach, Alex moved the other one to my hip, his hands guiding me to sway to the beat of the songs as our breaths became shallower and shallower.

"When I get you home…" he began, "I am going to devour you like no one has ever dared to devour you before."

Goosebumps broke out on my skin from the prospect of what was to come. "I can't wait that long. Just do it now. Take me now."

Biting my neck, he trailed kisses over my bare shoulder and across the exposed skin on my back. "Here?"

"Yes."

"In this club?"

"God, yes."

"In front of all these people?"

"We could slip somewhere darker—quieter."

"Fuck," he groaned, and I heard the pain in his voice—the way his words choked out and the conflict he was feeling between wanting to take me right there and then versus doing what was right. "No."

"Why not?"

"Because I love you too much to degrade you like that," he muttered, every word sounding like it held a silent groan of protest. "You're worth more."

I grinned and turned in his grip. My arms stayed around his neck, and I pushed my hips forward, pressing myself against him.

"And what if I wanted you to degrade me?" I taunted, raising a brow.

Alex's eyes closed for a second and he inhaled the longest breath, holding it in his chest before he let it out, his exhale heavy, loud and full of growl.

"No," he eventually croaked, opening his eyes.

"Not even if I do this?" I dropped my hand between us, slowly sliding it up and down his erection.

Alex's jaw set tight, the muscles twitching beneath his scruff as he shook his head slowly and narrowed his eyes. "Natalie, please."

I picked up my pace, feigning innocence as I batted my lashes and bit down on my lip.

"Nat, don't make me…"

"Making you take me is precisely what I'm trying to do."

He closed his eyes again, and his teeth ground together as he fought to stay in control. Alex could no longer hide the way his breathing was racing ahead of him, but the second he dropped his forehead against mine and I heard his voice crack, everything changed.

"Please," he begged roughly. "Don't. I can't do this in front of everybody. I wouldn't. Not with you."

It's amazing how you can feel so strong one moment, only to feel your desires and courage turn to dust in the hands of someone you love.

My arms slowly began to fall until they were hanging by my sides. I stayed frozen in place, mute and a little numb.

His forehead rolled against mine slowly, his nose brushing my nose, his hands sliding up and down my back soothingly.

"You're going to kill me," he groaned.

"Not with me?" I eventually whispered.

"What?"

"You said 'not with me.'"

His eyes pinged open, and he froze, too.

The confusion on his face was clear.

"What just happened?" he asked me.

I tried to be brave and swallow down my uncertainty, to not think about the kind of women he *would* do those things with, or had done those things with, but instead, I found myself repeating the three words that were ringing in my mind like a church bell on a Sunday morning. "Not with me."

Lifting himself away from me, Alex shook his head. "Don't let your mind go there. That's not what I meant, and you know it."

"No?" I croaked.

"Not even close—"

"I think I need to go to the bathroom."

"No. Nat, wait."

Pushing to move past him, I thought I'd made my escape until he moved in front of me to block my path. Lifting my chin up with a single finger, he pushed his nose to mine, once again, and he forced me to look straight into his eyes.

It hurt.

He hurt.

He was a mind-fucking concoction of everything I wanted to throw myself at and everything I was so damn afraid of losing again.

"You know you are different to every other woman out there. You know what you are to me. Do not turn what I feel for you into a negative thing."

I gave him a small nod, trying my hardest to look as though I'd already forgotten about it.

He shook his head and let me go, releasing a sigh of frustration of his own. "You're still a bad liar, babe."

"I need the bathroom." It was pathetic, but it was all I could say.

"I'll walk you over," he offered quietly.

"I'll be fine."

Before he could argue, I'd taken off in the direction of the toilets, my feet moving faster than felt natural as I weaved my way in and out of the bodies around me. The music was trying to drown out my every thought, but the truth was that my thoughts were so deeply rooted, stuck imagining the women he had been with who I probably wasn't going to match up to, that I felt like I was going to be sick.

I'd never been jealous with Marcus. Never.

This thing with Alex was making me feel crazy.

The thought of him being skin to skin with anybody who wasn't me, when it always should have been me, was making me ache. The alcohol I'd drunk that night only seemed to bring those vivid images to life even further until they were taunting me endlessly. No faces, just figures, pressing themselves against my Alex in dark corners, feeling him inside of them…

"Shit!" a voice cried the moment I charged straight into another body.

"I-I'm sorry," I squeaked, not looking up.

A pair of hands grabbed my arms, and it didn't take me long to realise that I'd been lucky enough to bump into Paul.

"Hey. What's going on? You okay?"

"Great." I cleared my throat quickly to try to sound more genuine. "Great. I just need the bathroom."

"Nat?" Paul ducked his head, bobbing it from side to side to try and catch my eyes. "Are you… crying?"

"No," I hit back, frowning as I tried to blink back the slight sheen of water that was blurring my vision.

"Bullshit. What the fuck has happened?"

"Nothing."

"It doesn't look like nothing."

"It is. It's just me. It's all me."

"What's you?"

"I think I'm having some kind of breakdown, drama queen moment, panic attack… I have no idea. It could be anything."

"This sounds like a job I'm not equipped to deal with."

Glancing around to make sure neither Suzie nor Alex could see us, I saw that the coast looked clear and began to pull Paul into a darker corner of the club.

"Paul, can I be honest with you?"

"It would help."

"I'm freaking out."

"Okay. Wanna tell me why?"

"I don't know how to put it into words. One minute I'm happy, the next I'm all over the place, trying to find the faults with this thing between Alex and me before he does, just so I'm prepared for when he leaves me this time."

"This time?"

"Yes."

"Are you fucking crazy?" he whispered.

My swallow of shame was harsh enough to hurt my throat. "Mainly just scared," I admitted quietly.

"What are you scared of, Nat?"

"I don't know." I panicked, looking down at my dress as I picked at it and spoke. "I guess I'm scared of something driving a wedge between us—something I have no control over. I'm scared of the secrets that are going to come out, and that I'm not going to be ready for them."

"Secrets? What kind of secrets? He's been honest with you about everything, hasn't he?"

"I don't know, Paul. You tell me. You're the one who told Suzie earlier that you bet he couldn't tell me all the names of the women he'd been with."

"Jesus, Nat, I was having a laugh. A joke. Trying to wind him up for being such a miserable shit when you weren't around. You're right. There are loads of stories about Alex you don't know, but none of them could hurt you. It's nothing anyone can use against you."

"Not even the women he slept with?"

He blinked slowly, and when Paul opened his eyes, he looked different. Like he knew before I did what this was really about. "Don't fuck this up because he had other women. That's not fair. You had Marcus."

"I know that." I frowned.

"Alex hasn't hidden anything from you. He's just chosen to spare you the details and not write a ten-thousand-word essay on all the positions he did with all the different bodies he used in all the different places he could get away with. Believe me—that's a love note from him you wouldn't want to read."

I cringed even harder, pushing my hands into my stomach where it felt like Paul had just stabbed me.

"This is just the booze messing with your head, Nat."

"I hope so"

Paul offered me a flat smile, bending his knees so our eyes were level when he spoke. "You miss that time with him?"

"More than I ever truly realised."

"He loves you… in a way I've never seen anyone love a woman before. It's powerful shit he's got stored inside that heart and mind of his, and every ounce of it is for you. Regardless of all those nightmares you're letting play out in your head, it's always been you. Since day one."

My head fell to one side as I let his words wash over me. "It's always been him for me. I think that's why I feel like this. The injustice of it all, the fact that I know life is short, and I've lost so much time with him—time that should have been ours. Time that belonged to us that I can't get back."

"Then quit wasting even more time with me when you could be with him. Let it go. What more is there that matters? You can't know everything. You think Suzie doesn't want to know every secret I have?"

"You have secrets?"

Paul laughed. "Those who say they don't are full of shit. Suzie would love nothing more than to know every dark thought I've ever had—every little thing I've ever kept from her. When you love someone, you want to crawl under their skin and set up camp in their mind, right? But, sweetheart, that just isn't realistic. Alex is human. He's thought bad things about himself and lives with more regret than any twenty-two-year-old on this planet. He's made hundreds of mistakes, and if I know him like I think I know him, he'll make a hundred more before the week is out." He sighed, running his hand down my cheek as we stared at one another. "Answer me this: has he done everything he can to spoil you since he found you again?"

"Everything and more."

"And he tells you he loves you?"

"Like every time is the first time."

"Then stop trying to find problems that aren't there. Live for today, for fuck's sake, woman. You've already said it yourself: life is too short. Time is too precious and all that fluffy shit." He dropped his hand, pushing it into his pocket. "Maybe he's even more scared than you, have you ever thought of that? Maybe he's scared to tell you all the sordid things you seem so desperate to know in case you end up seeing him the way he's seen himself for too long, and you run away from him like you just have done."

Damn.

"Paul?"

"Yeah?"

"Why didn't you ever tell me how much you guys had stayed in touch?"

"Because he begged me not to and he's my friend. I respected his decisions and choices, even if I didn't agree with them."

"What about mine?" I asked, aware that my face was showing a little bit of the betrayal I was feeling. "What about my choice to love a man who I had no idea still loved me? What about my choice to help him? To not miss out on five years with my soul mate?" I didn't feel like myself as an anger, a frustration that I hadn't been aware was lurking inside of me began to take over. "What about my choices, Paul? Seems like everyone respected Alex's decisions, thinking they were best for me, but not one of you thought to let me choose for myself. None of you except Marcus."

Paul scoffed quickly, raising a brow as he rocked on the heels of his feet and looked away from me. "If you think Marcus gave you any fucking choice in all of this, you're sadly mistaken." He laughed a humourless laugh before his eyes met mine again. "I mean, damn it, Natalie, I liked the guy, but if one single person took your choices away from you, it was that dude."

"W-what?" I pushed out a little breathlessly.

"You have no idea."

"Paul, what did Marcus do?"

"It doesn't matter."

"Yes, it does. Tell me. You just said that he—"

"That's enough!" Alex's voice boomed beside us, forcing our heads to swing in his direction as he appeared out of nowhere.

His frown was heavy as he glared at Paul, the warning on his features visible enough for me to see clearly.

Paul immediately looked like he'd been caught smoking by his mum.

"Shit," he muttered.

Alex's hand reached out for mine, and even though he was glaring at Paul with a look I knew was capable of hurting his friend, I took it. I took his hand, sliding my fingers between his because I, too, was ashamed at being caught out talking about Alex and my darkest fears to someone other than him.

Alex's jaw was tight, and his eyes were narrowed as he stared at Paul.

"I think we're going to head back to the hotel, Paul," he eventually ground out. "Tell Suzie we're sorry for slipping out. We'll speak to her tomorrow."

"Listen, man. I didn't mean to—"

A pointed look from Alex had him stopping in his tracks, and I watched as the two of them said so much to each other without actually saying a single word.

"No problem. We'll catch up with you guys tomorrow," Paul eventually said.

"Wait," I dared myself to say, wrapping my free hand around Alex's wrist and angling my body so that I was pressing up against him. "Did you hear us?"

He looked down at me from the corners of his eyes. "We should go."

"I *asked* you if you heard us, Alex."

"I heard enough."

I glanced at Paul who looked suitably guilty before I turned my attention back to Alex. "You know what he meant, don't you? You guys are holding another secret back from me and it's to do with Marcus."

In my peripheral vision, I saw Paul drop his head into his hand and leave it there while Alex continued to look at me.

"Alex," I pleaded. "Please. I'm so tired of not knowing everything. Just tell me."

His eyes closed before I felt his body relax next to mine. I didn't want to fall out, but I had a feeling that was exactly what was about to happen. There were too many things I didn't know, and as Alex closed his eyes in resignation, I hoped with my entire heart that he realised that in order for us to move forward, there was no avoiding the fact that we were going to have to go back for a while.

"Fine, but not here. Let's go," Alex ordered quietly.

TWELVE

We took the stairs to our hotel room, and I tried not to think about how much history was repeating itself for us in one night. A fall out in a nightclub. Those dark, quiet taxi rides home. The stairwell of a hotel.

The only question left was… how would our night end?

The light above the key card flashed green, allowing us access to our room, and as he pushed the door open for me, I stared at that green light with the word *go* blaring out in my mind.

Go.

Make the first move. Be the leader for once. New beginnings. Old fights.

I dropped my bag on top of the nightstand and turned to face him, watching as he ran his hand over the back of his neck.

I folded my arms across my chest. "Are you ready to tell me everything that you're keeping from me?"

"Are you sure you want to do this?"

"Only if you're going to give me the facts about everything, because otherwise, what's the point?"

"You think I lie to you?" He scowled, clearly offended.

"I think you omit a lot of truths. It's the same thing, isn't it?"

"Doesn't that work both ways?" Alex challenged, suddenly copying my pose. His hands folded across his chest, accentuating the muscles in his arms, and he widened his legs to balance himself.

"I've been honest with you," I hit back.

"Oh, yeah?" He smirked, his eyes flashing with a challenge. "So, you were honest before when you said you needed to use the bathroom at the club, and you weren't just using it as an excuse to get as far away from me as you could so we didn't have to actually talk, you know, like two grown adults are meant to, right?"

I blinked, buying myself some time. "I needed to think. You'd just poured cold water over a hot body by telling me that I was the one person you couldn't go wild with."

"What a way to twist my words, Nat."

"Don't tell me that's not what you meant."

"You clearly have no idea what I meant."

"No. Because you never tell me anything *real*," I strained out.

"Everything I tell you is real. Every goddamn thing."

"Then why wouldn't you touch me the way I wanted to be touched in that club? Why did you say, *Not with you* the way you said it?"

"Because," he croaked, pausing to suck in a deep breath. "Because I've done too many things with too many people I don't remember in too many dark corners. That's why. You are not one of those women, Natalie. You are better. You deserve more."

"So we can never do anything, I don't know, seedy or dangerous together because you think I'm too fragile? That I'm not as daring as those other girls were?"

"I tell you that I love you and respect you too much to use your body for a cheap moment of gratification in front of complete strangers who could be all kinds of fucking freaky, dirty and sick, and you see it as me saying that I don't want to have a good time with you?"

"That's exactly how I saw it." I nodded sharply, unashamed to admit what I was thinking. I'd been considerate, reasonable, and controlled my whole damn life. For once, just once, I wanted to throw all of my ugliness out there and watch to see if he stuck around. I took a step closer to him, but we were still six feet apart. There was a tension keeping that distance between us. I was glad for it… for now. "I'm saying that I think you might still see me as the weak little girl you used to have to look out for on a bus, and maybe, just maybe I'm not that person anymore. I've grown up because I've had to. I've learned to survive, to be a little bit reckless and wild every now and again. And maybe, just maybe, I want cheap as much as the next girl. Or the last girl."

"The last girl?" His brows rose high. Alex ran his tongue over his bottom lip before dragging it through his teeth and shaking his head. "Damn. You really are going to do this, aren't you?"

I shrugged lightly. "I guess I am."

"You're going to make me feel even more guilty for trying to live when I thought you'd gone forever."

"And why do you feel guilty?" My voice shook. "Is it because you screwed so many of them that you don't even know their names? Tell me, Alex. Tell me why. Tell me right now—"

"You goddamn know why! Because they weren't you!" he bellowed like he was in pain.

"Alex." I flinched.

"No, you want to do this then let's do this. Let's lay all our cards on the table and get our shit out there. What do you need to know?"

"Nothing. I don't know. *Every*thing!"

"Everything? You sure, Natalie? You want all the sordid, dirty, disgusting details that sometimes wake me up in the middle of the night just to fill me with shame? You want me to relive the moments that make me feel sick when I think about them? Is that what you want from me?" He began to shake, physically shake, and his muscles tensed even more, straining against the black edges of his polo shirt. "You want to know how many, you want to know where, you want to know what I said to them or didn't say, is that it? Is that really how you want to start this new beginning of ours? Why? Why are you trying to ruin this when you know how much I fucking love you?"

"Maybe because I feel like there's so much I don't know about you, and others know you better, and I hate that. Maybe… maybe I don't know why."

"Own your shit, Nat. Spit it out. I'm not leaving this hotel room, no matter how much you want rid of me, until you get it all off your chest, once and for all."

"I can't."

"Okay. Then, let me say it for you. You're too afraid to admit that you blame me for everything, don't you? You feel it, deep down in the pit of your stomach, that while you love me, you also still hate me because you blame me. It's my fault we were apart for five years. It's my fault that I wasn't man enough to step up and be what you needed me to be. It's my fault you missed out on us—that *we* missed out on us. I know it is. Those mistakes are mine. Hey, I'm cool with admitting it. I own my shit. Maybe it's time you stopped trying to protect me and admit that you blame me, too," he practically spat out.

The truth of what he'd said had my eyes flying open as I lunged forward and jabbed my finger in my own chest.

"I *do* blame you!" I shouted. "I blame you. I blame myself. I blame your father. I blame my parents. I blame our friends… *all of them!* I'm scared I'm going to blame Marcus, too, after what Paul said at the club. I blame every single one of you for taking *you* away from me, and I know what happened can't ever be erased, but now that I've let you back into my heart so fully, I have to think about all those other women who have had you, and it kills me a little bit inside whenever I imagine it."

"Then don't imagine it!" he snapped back, his arms opening up and flying out to the sides.

"How do I stop? Paul knows everything you did when I wasn't around. Your history is always going to be there. I'm on pins waiting and wondering what smartass comment he's going to mutter about you next that I don't understand. I have no idea what's going to have me irrationally churned up next, and I hate it. I hate feeling like something is going to come along and make me lose you again."

"You think I could ever walk away from you again?"

"Maybe. I…"

"Let me make one thing clear. That is never going to happen. Not unless you beg me to leave you because you no longer love me. And even then it would take a whole army to remove me from your life."

"How can you be sure? How can either of us be sure?"

"Because without you, I have nothing to live for anymore." Alex took a careful step closer, shortening the space between us. "Listen to me. Paul is a dickhead—I know that more than anyone—but he was there for me when I needed someone to talk to. He's always been there for me. You can at least understand that, surely?"

"It should have been me!" I cried without reservation, jabbing my chest again. "Don't you see? It should… have been… me. Me you spoke to. Me you screwed senseless. Me you used to numb the pain of what was going on with your parents. All of it should have been me!" I practically choked on the last word, and my body gave in, my shoulders falling forward as my head rolled and I glared down at the carpet. "I should have been there so you didn't have to make those mistakes—so neither of us had to make any mistakes we would have to live with for the rest of our lives," I whispered.

Alex didn't move or say anything, but I could feel his own pain rolling off of him in waves.

"Five years. We lost five years," I whispered.

"I wasn't right for you back then."

"Yes, you were."

A silence hung over us for quite some time before he dared to break it.

"The last thing I ever want to be to you is a disappointment, Natalie."

"The only person I'm disappointed in right now is myself," I assured him, looking up through heavy eyes. "I never realised I would feel this much resentment over losing you once I finally had you."

"Resentment towards who?"

"Everyone, and I don't know how to get rid of it now that it's here."

"I'm terrified to ask you this question, but I need you to be honest with me if I'm making you miserable. Do you want me to get out of here? To leave you alone for a while to, I don't know, clear your head?"

My face scrunched up tightly at the very thought of him leaving me again. "No," I said with absolute, soul-crushing certainty. "I will never, ever want that, but I also don't want to pretend with you. Not here in London. Not tomorrow over breakfast with Paul and Suzie. Not while we travel the world, not when we resettle back home, and not even when we're old, grey and all wrung out. I need you to see me for who I am. I can't pretend again, no matter how ugly my truths are. I need to pour this out, set it free. I need to see myself for who I am, and as it turns out, I'm a bitter, resentful fool who just wants…" I stopped, not able to say anything else as both my mouth and my mind dried up completely.

Alex took another step closer. "Tell me. Tell me what the hell you want from me and I will give it to you."

"I want the impossible."

"Tell me…"

"I want the past gone," I admitted quietly as I glanced up at him. "I want that time with you back, and now that I know just how good we are together, I can't help it—I feel even more robbed and cheated of what we could have been."

"Do you even hear what you are asking of me?" he wheezed out. "Do you think I don't want the same thing, every single second of every single day. I dream of that shit when I'm asleep. It's all I've ever thought about, and something I, *we*, have to live with for the rest of our lives. But we're together now, and I'll be damned if I'm going to let that change."

I gulped quietly, knowing he was right, but the alcohol had invaded my heart and my mind, making it impossible for me to stop speaking without reservation.

"How did you do it?" I asked him quietly.

"Do what?"

"Sleep with all those women while you loved me?"

"That's not fair." He blanched.

"Tell me," I begged him softly.

"I don't know, Nat. I just did it. How would you feel if I asked you how you loved two men at once?"

"I did what I had to do to try to forget you because I didn't know you still wanted me."

"And you were the only one who was allowed to turn to their coping mechanism?" he whispered. "You don't think I feel like I've got a mountain to climb to compete with Marcus on an emotional level. You don't think I know how much everyone loves him? How people wanted him to win."

"Win? I'm not a prize."

"You are. You really, really are. You're the best damn prize any man could ever wish to win. He knew that. I knew that. Everyone knew except you."

"It doesn't matter what everyone else wanted. It was always you for me," I assured him quietly.

"That doesn't make it any easier. I look at how much you've grown, how you've changed, how much confidence you have now, and I know that's all down to him, not me. It twists me up knowing it was him. Marcus stepped up, and I couldn't be more grateful, despite what he…" Alex trailed off, a flash of panic washing over his face.

"Despite?" I pressed.

"It doesn't matter."

"This is what I'm talking about. What happened that I don't know about?"

It all proved too much for him. Alex dropped down to the edge of the bed, clearly tired and worn out. His hands fell between his parted legs while his sigh burst heavily from his lips.

"This is difficult for me. I know I shouldn't care because he's your ex-boyfriend, but I do, and I don't want you to think badly of him."

"If we've learned anything from all of this, please let it be that I should be free to make up my own mind about people and their actions."

"Fine." He rubbed his forehead in worry. "Do you remember when we sat in that bar in Leeds just a few weeks ago, and the first thing you told me was that Marcus didn't mind if we stayed friends? That Marcus wasn't worried about me being in your life?"

I remembered it clearly. I remembered the look of surprise on Alex's face when I told him. "Yes."

He glanced up at me with worry in his eyes. "I was surprised to hear you say that and believe that it could be anywhere close to the truth."

"Why wouldn't it be the truth?"

Spinning around until his legs were in front of me, Alex took hold of my hands and pulled on them until I was standing between his parted legs, looking down on him. "He hated me, Nat."

"He didn't know you." I scowled.

"We've met before."

"When?"

"That night after you went to see my mum at our house, and you walked away forever, everything changed. I got home from the club to find Mum was waiting up for me. She told me everything that had been said between the two of you. I asked her if you'd been alone, and she told me there had been someone waiting for you in the back of a cab. I knew straight away who it was, that it was Marcus. All I could think about and imagine were his hands on you in that club and how he looked at you the way I looked at you. I knew then that it was over between us and that you'd have someone else to lean on. I no longer had any rights over you, especially because it was my fault that you were hurting in the first place.

"Marcus saw you in a horrible state that I, *me*, not anyone else, had put you in. He had a right to be angry with me. He was the one who held you while you cried and made you better. If I'd been in his shoes, I'd have done the same thing he did."

"What same thing?"

"He came to see me the next morning."

My eyes widened. "No, he didn't."

"Yeah, he did," he said quietly. "He came back to the house and he was pissed off."

"No…"

"He'd spent the whole night consoling you, Natalie, and he was angry."

"Did he hurt you?"

"Not really."

"And what the hell does *that* mean?"

"It means that we were two guys who clearly had feelings for the same girl, and he wanted to make it known that he had your back. I knew who he was, and I remember looking down at his hands while he spoke. All I could think was *those touched my girl last night*. I wanted to hate him the very moment I saw him, and from the moment he grabbed my shirt and slammed me up against my door. But as soon as he started talking, I knew that he was going to be the guy who would make things better for you. He was angry. Furious. It was obvious he cared. He had his other fist balled by his side and I knew it was taking every bit of control he possessed not to hit me. Hell, I even wanted him to hit me. I knew I could take it." Alex carefully pulled my hand away from my mouth, entwining it with his, once again. "When I heard his warning to stay away from you, I was grateful in a way. It meant I'd have someone there to stop me if I ever selfishly tried to drag you back under."

"Marcus told you to stay away from me?"

"No." He shook his head. "He said that if I cared about you in any way, let alone loved you, then I *should* stay away. He was right, but what took me a while to realise is that he was wrong, too. I shouldn't have left you, Nat. He thought I was just another player. He had no clue how much I fucking loved you. No one did. You have no idea how desperate I was to run to your house, burst through the door, charge up those stairs and scoop you up into my arms while I poured all of my apologies over your body. No idea, baby. It was a physical ache. My feet itched to take off so many times, and all my hands ever did was miss you. But Marcus did the right thing. He reminded me that I wasn't ready for you, and that I'd only break you even more until there was no way to put you back together again."

All of my mixed emotions were jumping over one another to try and be heard. "He had no right. None of you did."

"I know that now. He'll know that now. He might have known it all along. A part of me thinks that's why he was always so reasonable with you about me. I guess he always knew that if you found out what he'd done, you'd blame him, and he'd lose you anyway."

"All this time…" My voice trailed off.

"He was trying to protect you."

I looked up and over Alex's head, remembering each moment Marcus had been incredibly reasonable about Alex and my past. Right up until Paul and Suzie's wedding…

My eyes found Alex's again. "That night at Suzie and Paul's wedding, when I saw you two together on the dance floor… he was reminding you to stay away, wasn't he?"

"Can you blame him? You were there. You felt that spark between us, stronger than ever. It was at that wedding that I realised, truly realised, that I was willing to cross every line to get you back. I think I already knew it before then. It was why I came back to Leeds. But seeing Paul and Suzie, speaking to them and knowing that I wanted with you what they had with each other… I dropped all my masks that night. Paul was constantly on my case, telling me not to let you slip through my fingers. He reminded me how Marcus could ask you to marry him any day, and once that was done, I was out of the race forever. When I saw you at Paul and Suzie's wedding, I just knew I couldn't be nice about it anymore. I wanted you. Marcus must have seen it. He did see it. I think a part of him was more afraid of you finding out what he'd done than him losing you."

"I'm going to kill him," I mouthed silently.

Alex allowed a little smile to slip before he shook his head and released a small laugh. "No, you're not."

"Oh, I really am."

"Why would you do that? The man was a fucking hero."

"And how do you figure that?" I asked, not finding anything particularly funny. I was too numb from even more revelations to think or feel anything other than confused.

"He stepped up. He put his whole life on hold to keep you safe and me away."

I *had* been safe with Marcus. I'd felt safer with him than I had in my whole life. There was no fear of losing something that would shatter my world. All I ever worried about was hurting him, and maybe that was how I should have known he deserved better than I could have given him.

Or at least he had before I found out what he'd done.

I took a step back from Alex and watched as his face fell.

"I was safer, but I wasn't happier."

"I know that now, but if you'll let me, I'll never let you be unhappy again."

"Until someone else asks you to stay away from me?"

He opened his mouth to speak, but clearly thought better of it, choosing instead to pull me back to him.

"First your dad, then Marcus. What if someone else comes

along and tells you you're no good for me. Are you going to go? Walk away, despite knowing how much I love you and want you in my life?"

He wrapped his arms around me, but we could both feel the tension and hurt in my body.

"I'm not going anywhere, and I'm not going to let you do to me what I did to you back then, Nat. I won't let you push me away."

I was too tired and full of alcohol to think straight. My head fell to his and my body went limp in his arms. The strength he held in his hands pressed into my back as he ran soothing lines up and down it.

He was here.

We were together.

Everything I'd ever dreamed about was in my grip, and here I was, acting like I'd never acted before, creating arguments that didn't need to be had because I wasn't sure how to deal with this imbalance of swirling emotions that were taking over.

"Do you remember that night in the park when you told me you weren't pregnant?"

I nodded my head against his.

"I saw it then, that look you had in your eyes. That hurt you felt when you thought I didn't care. Do you want to know what that was? That was disappointment. That was the end of it for me because I knew I no longer had a selfish reason to keep you in my life. A small part of me was hoping we'd have a reason to stay together, just so I could quit thinking of excuses to leave you."

"You wanted me to be pregnant?"

"Yes. No. No for you and yes for me. I was torn up about what I should do. I kind of wanted the decision to be taken out of my hands. I wanted us tied together forever, and I was an idiot who, for just a moment, thought a possible baby was the only way it would happen."

"A part of me was disappointed, too," I admitted quietly. "I knew you were slipping away. I felt cheap because of those thoughts. Who wants a baby to keep a man?"

"A woman who loves him more than he deserves to be loved."

"Let's go with that." I grinned half-heartedly.

Alex's smile matched mine for a brief second before he exhaled loudly and searched my eyes. "I just want to move forward with you, and I know I'm going to make mistakes along the way. Big fucking mistakes, Nat. I'm not good at this. I never was."

I pushed my fingers through his hair, watching as his eyes closed briefly and a small moan rumbled in the back of his throat. "I want to move forward, too."

"How do we start to do that if you can't accept that our pasts are what they are?" Alex looked back up at me. "They're back there, long gone. We can't forget them, but I don't want them to destroy any future we have together."

"They won't," I reassured him quietly.

"How can I be sure?"

"Because…" I paused and sucked in a breath, feeling the memories of my sister's last words flowing through me. "I made a promise to Lizzy to never let the end of one thing stop me from enjoying the beginning of another. So, just because one thing between us ended back then, it doesn't mean I should let this new thing, this better thing, burn out before it even has a chance to start."

"There she is," he said through a dopey smile. "Lizzy never lets me down."

My brows rose. "She doesn't?"

"Who do you think I spoke to about you for five years?"

"I thought it was Paul."

"He got the bloke stuff. Lizzy… she got the truth from me in the middle of the night, or when I was so drunk I could barely remember if I was alive and talking to her, or whether I'd finally crossed over to where she was."

"What did you talk to her about?"

"Everything. The truth. All the stuff I couldn't admit to myself but found easy to tell her. Like how sorry I was for letting you down—for letting her down. I told her how much I loved you. I told her to make sure Marcus treated you right. I thanked her for somehow bringing you to me."

"You believe she was responsible for it?"

He huffed out a small laugh before he fell onto his back, pulling me down ever so gently until I was lying on top of him where I belonged.

"Yeah. Maybe, but I guess I believe your sister will always find a way to make us be together. Whether it's true or not, I don't know, but I choose to believe that she's guiding us. I choose to believe she's making us see what will truly make us happy, even before we know what that is for ourselves."

I stared into his eyes, wondering how it was possible for him to speak of my sister like he'd known her his whole life, and for it not to seem in any way weird to me. I leaned down until my lips brushed over his and our breaths mingled together.

"I choose you, Alex. I choose our own happy."

"I choose happy," he repeated with a smile.

"No more looking back."

THIRTEEN

Despite my exhaustion, we didn't fall asleep straight away. After lying in silence on Alex's chest for some time after we'd finished talking, with his fingers running languidly through my hair, I finally allowed myself to speak.

"I love you."

He didn't answer me instantly, but the deep intake of breath and the rise of his chest that moved me with him had me smiling.

"Are you happy?" I asked softly.

"Yep," he answered roughly before he pressed his lips to the top of my head.

"Good."

Alex ran the tip of his nose over my hair before he lifted a hand and ran his fingers through it, fisting it tightly behind the back of my neck and causing goosebumps to flare to life.

"I love you," he told me. "Despite you being a bit of a fishwife."

Blinking a couple of times, I eventually forced my eyes open, and laughter bubbled in my chest around the same time it bubbled in his. "At least now I know what it feels like to really be jealous of someone."

"Not a great feeling, is it?"

I rested my arms over his chest and let my chin fall against them as I looked up at him. "I don't know. There's an element of comfort in jealousy. It means I finally have something in my life that I'm passionate about—that I'm desperate to hold on to."

"That's one way to look at it."

"I'm finding all the silver linings from now on. I want this life with you to be so bright."

***

"I just want to apologi–"

My hand shot up in the air before I turned to Paul and gave him the stink eye. He'd been following me around all morning, telling me he'd been out of order the night before, assuring me he hadn't meant to cause any offence.

"For the love of God, Paul, how many more times do I have to tell you? You have nothing to apologise for."

"I know, I know," he said sheepishly as he pushed both his hands into the pockets of his jeans and rocked back and forth on the balls of his feet.

"Suzie told you off last night, didn't she?"

"Fuck, yeah." He nodded, looking up at me through his lashes, unable to hide the adoration he had for his wife as it shone from his eyes.

We were currently standing in the luscious grounds of Kenwood House in Hampstead Heath, the sun shining down on the almost white building that stood proudly on the hill beside us. Suzie had begged Paul to bring her here, apparently having had him trail all around London to visit every location spot they used while filming *Notting Hill*. After very little effort, both she and Paul had convinced Alex and I to go along with them.

Suzie and Alex were sprawled out on a large picnic blanket we'd brought along, while Paul and I had gone to get coffees from the small cafe that was there for visitors of the huge mansion.

Turning back to the counter where our drinks sat waiting, I picked two up and waited for Paul to do the same. I took off, walking back towards my boyfriend and one of my best friends as the sun beat down on my ever-smiling face.

I heard Paul catching up to me from behind.

"I just don't want you to think I'm not proud as shit of you both because no one is as ecstatic as I am about you two hooking back up. This is what Suzie and I have been wanting to happen since forever."

Stopping in my tracks, I turned to look at him. "Paul, listen to me. Are you listening? Last night, I don't know what happened, but I assure you for the hundredth time, it wasn't you. It wasn't Suzie. It wasn't even Alex. It was me! All of it was me."

Paul scowled, looking genuinely confused.

"All I've ever wanted is Alex. When I got him, I guess I was afraid of losing him again. It freaked me out. I panicked. It was like, with you guys here, our pasts were catching up with this new bubble I'd created for us down here, and I didn't like it."

"You didn't want us here?"

"That's not what I'm saying." I shook my head. "I'm just saying that a part of me felt like you were here to take him away from me again. It was irrational and it was stupid–"

"Very fucking stupid," he interrupted.

"Epically fucking stupid," I agreed. "But one minute he was just mine and the next minute you were there reminding me that he'd had other women, reminding me he'd done things, seen things, been places, all of which I didn't know anything about. I didn't know he could sing or play the piano. He's got so many layers, he's like a damn onion. It shook me up a little bit. You reminded me that we're still fragile. What Alex showed me when we got back to our hotel room is that it's okay for us to be fragile still. Maybe we'll be this way for a while. Maybe we'll always be this way. But we're together, we're happy, and I have to learn to love him for who he is now—who he's grown to be. Just as he has to do with me."

"That's deep, Nat." Paul leaned in closer, placing a small kiss on my cheek before he moved his mouth to my ear and whispered, "Don't ever let anyone tell you that you aren't the most epic girl that exists. Besides my wife, of course."

My cheeks blushed in embarrassment. "Jeez, Paul. Anyone would think you cared about me."

He pulled back and laughed freely. "Care about you? I love the shit out of you, woman. You should know that by now."

"I love you, too," I told him a little shyly.

"Well, that takes care of that then."

"I guess it does." I smiled.

When we turned around to look at Alex and Suzie, we saw them both sitting there with their arms folded over their chests and accusatory glares on their faces.

"Uh-oh," Paul mumbled.

"She saw you whispering to me, didn't she?"

"And the kiss on the cheek."

"Are you about to get your arse handed to you on a plate?"

Paul shrugged. "At least we'll have something to eat for

lunch if I do."

FOURTEEN

We said our goodbyes to Suzie and Paul after lunch. They had to get back to their everyday lives where they hoped to buy a new house, set up camp and probably, someday in the not too distant future, start a family.

They were twenty-two going on fifty. Their love was solid, built on a foundation of unshakable stone where no doubt or cloud could ever cast a shadow over them, and nobody else's opinion could ever matter.

It was beautiful to watch.

After leaving our friends, we headed back into London and, hand in hand, wandered the streets aimlessly, in no rush to be anywhere as long as we were side by side. The sun was getting lower in the sky, and the entire city appeared to be mellow for once.

We hardly spoke, the two of us. It reminded me of those times on the bus all over again—the subtle glances at one another, the small smiles, the blood rushing to my cheeks, and the air held tight in my chest whenever he looked at me and made me forget how to breathe.

We ate ice cream as we wandered, and I got butterflies in my stomach whenever Alex reached over to gently brush away a stray hair from my cheek or wipe away raspberry sauce from the corner of my mouth. I felt his love whenever we went to cross a busy road and his fingers squeezed mine that little bit tighter than before. I smiled whenever he held a door open for me. I became overexcited whenever he would move behind my body and his hand would slide over my arse before giving it a teasing squeeze. His smirk made me melt. His jaw made me rigid with lust. His eyes—those swoonworthy hazel eyes—reminded me that as long as I could see them, I was home.

Before long, we'd wandered into the middle of Clapham Common, and as the sun slowly began to set on our day, leaving only a few hardcore runners and dog walkers lingering in the park, I felt a peace settle over me that was becoming more familiar than ever.

As we approached the bandstand and I told Alex how beautiful its silhouette looked against the backdrop of the yellow and orange sky, his body turned, and he guided me up the steps until the two of us were standing in the middle of it.

Just us…

And the sound of the birds above us singing their songs of freedom.

I stepped away from Alex, my serene smile feeling dopey on my face as I made a small circle with my footsteps and took a full turn to look around. There was something about the place—

something about the atmosphere mixed with the colours in the sky—that had me feeling like I was standing in the middle of Heaven.

Alex watched me, his hands deep in his pockets and his smile reaching right up to his eyes. I wanted to run to him and throw myself into his arms, but I couldn't take my attention away from the trees, the people, the lonely bench that sat in front of the bandstand where I imagined many couples kissing, many children falling onto, and many a stranger watching the world go by.

If you looked closely enough, you could virtually see all the things Clapham Common had seen in its lifetime.

"Isn't it magnificent here?" My arms spun out in a circle, and I dropped my head back between my shoulders and closed my eyes.

"The view doesn't get better than this," Alex replied quietly.

Opening my eyes, I grinned and came to a stop, feeling the mid length, pale blue skirt I was wearing wrap itself around my calves. "I was talking about the grounds and the actual scenery, not your view of me."

"I haven't looked at any of that yet. I'm preoccupied."

"What could possibly be more beautiful than all of this?" I challenged.

"You."

I laughed softly, letting my chin fall to my chest for just a moment before I pushed my blonde hair behind my ears and made my way over to him.

Wrapping my arms around his neck, I stood on tiptoes so our eyes were as level as I could get them. "Let's end it here."

"End what here?" He frowned slightly, his arms coming around me as his hands found their resting place on my arse.

"This part of our adventure."

"You want to leave?"

"I'm ready to move on to new places with you. I'm ready to go and discover the whole world. I'm ready to find more shops for us to buy tacky gifts from. I'm ready to swim in oceans and to roll around in the sand. I'm ready to find new parks, new grass for us to talk about Mexican food versus Italian. More teenage conversations of wolves versus eagles. I'm ready to live five lost years with you in just a month if I have to."

Alex pulled one of my hands down between us while keeping his other hand firmly on my bottom. In one simple movement, he had me in his grip like he was about to take the lead with me in a waltz.

"More bandstands for us to dance in," he said softly.

"You dance, too?"

"Full package, baby."

He began to guide us round the bandstand in a slow dance that I had no idea I could actually do before I was doing it. It wasn't fancy. It wasn't anything more than a few sidesteps here and there while he pressed his chest against mine and guided me to where he wanted me to be, but it was intense. It was an intimacy I'd never felt, and it was a dream come true.

I was a girl dancing to the sounds of silence, with her favourite boy in her arms, her whole future ahead of her and for once, excitement for the life the two of them were about to create together.

It didn't matter where he'd been or what he'd done. It didn't matter where we were or where we were going to go. All that mattered to me was the company I was going to keep.

"Let's go to Greece," Alex whispered in my ear.

"Then Thailand."

"Maybe on to Italy after that?"

"Oh, Rome." I sighed wistfully.

"Together." He smiled. "And one day, the two of us will

come back here to Clapham Common. We'll walk back into this bandstand, and I'll watch you throw your arms out and spin in a circle with a smile on your face as you close your eyes and remember this moment right here."

"I'd like that."

"Only next time there'll be one difference." Alex dropped his forehead against mine. "Next time, while you're spinning and I'm admiring, I'll reach into my pocket and I'll pull out a small box with a ring inside."

My muscles tensed in his grip.

"A ring?" I whispered. His huff of laughter had me freezing completely, bringing us both to a standstill.

"*The* ring," he told me confidently. "And I'll get down on one knee, never taking my eyes off of you as you get lost in your own head. Eventually, my silence will make you pause and open your beautiful blue eyes. For a second, you'll panic and think I've left you, but then you'll look down and see me smiling the biggest, proudest smile of my life as I look up at you from bended knee and ask you to marry me."

Tears formed in my eyes. Something locked inside of me. Something secured itself. Something clicked and crashed into my heart, letting me know that even the thought of Alex proposing to me felt so right it could never be questioned by anyone or anything. A part of me wanted it to happen right now. For him to do it—to tie us together. I was that certain he was who I wanted and needed to spend the rest of my living days with.

"I'll tell you all the things I love about you before you say yes. I'll watch as you cry and clasp a hand over your mouth. I'll make you a lot of promises that I intend to keep. And then, eventually, hopefully, if my current good luck with you sticks around for a while longer..." He stopped and exhaled slowly, reaching up to wipe a stray happy tear from my cheek before looking back into my eyes. "You'll say—"

"Yes," I finished for him.

"Yes," he breathed out through a lazy smile.

"Yes, yes, yes."

"Without any reservations whatsoever."

"None at all," I assured him with a shaky voice.

"But not yet. We've got a lifetime to look forward to."

"Bring it on." I smiled.

"I love you, Natalie Vincent. Always have, always will."

"Always have," I repeated softly, "Always will."

He began to dance with me again, our foreheads never breaking contact as we stared into each other's eyes and remained silent. Everything that needed to be said had already been spoken.

We had a bright future to look forward to. We had so many high times to enjoy, and no doubt we had low times ahead of us, too, and we'd need to lean on each other for support. It was true that I'd admired Paul and Suzie's love for one another. I always would. But as I danced around the bandstand with the love of *my* life, I realised that no two loves were the same, and that was okay. I was finally realising what mine and Alex's love really was, after all this time.

Ours was a softly spoken love. A *not everything needs to be said out loud* love. An *I can't breathe without him* kind of love. The *I need him and he needs me* love. The *you appeared out of nowhere and brought me to life* love. The *we're the only thing that keeps the other one going* kind of love. The *growing old together* love. The *nothing hidden* love. The *magnetic* kind of love. The *there's no way of avoiding it* kind of love.

The forever love.

Our trials and tribulations got us there, and I'd never been more grateful for all the storms we'd had to pass through to finally find our paradise.

Now all that was left for me to do was live and be happy.

With Alex.

Always Alex.

We were Natexus.

PLAYLIST

Creep – Radiohead

Ain't No Use – Matt Woods

Waiting – Aquilo

You've Got That Way – Liz Longley

I Was Made For Loving You – Kina Grannis

A Thousand Years – Jasmine Thompson

Great Escape – Jasmine Thompson

Like I'm Gonna Lose You – Jasmine Thompson

River – Leon Bridges

Hope For Now – City and Colour

Beautiful Birds – Passenger (feat. Birdy)

All I Want – Dawn Golden

Cavalier – James Vincent McMorrow

Reflection – Liv Dawson

I Can't Go On Without You – Kaleo

I Choose You – Rebecca Ferguson

Available to follow on SPOTIFY

ACKNOWLEDGMENTS

As always, it takes a village.

Of course, my thanks always go to Lou Stock. Wilma. Weezy. That friend of mine that doesn't let me lay down, roll over, and quit. That person that, even when I'm trying not to let the rest of the world see I'm struggling, somehow seems to know and swoops right in with a Rocky quote to pick me back up. She does every single graphic for every single book I've ever done, and I trust her with my life.

Claire Allmendinger, thank you for always being there for me, both as a friend and an editor.

Wendy Shatwell.

Thank you for creating Bare Naked Words and for all you and Claire do for me.

Family and Friends

It's really hard for me to keep listing you all in these acknowledgements of mine, but let me just say that if you've ever offered me even a single word of encouragement, no matter who you are, what way you offered it, or how often we speak, trust me when I say you are worth your weight in gold. I didn't truly know what I was getting myself into with this writing malarkey. I never knew how lonely it could be, how crippling the self-doubt was, or how one tiny bad comment can bring months of hard work to a halt. Those moments where you've picked me up with an encouraging smile, a tap on the shoulder or even a 'You got this, Vic' – they help me more than I can explain. So, thank you. My life would be shitty without you.

Readers and Bloggers

I am nothing without you. It's that simple.

CPCCH Unit

I really am nothing without you. One day, imma take y'all to DisneyLand. *nods* Thanks for putting up with me. My love for you isn't something I can put into words.

Grandad Jim, Grandma Bess.

The greatest love story I ever did see.

I miss you both. So much, it hurts.

Hope I'm making you proud... despite the sex scenes and foul language.

 Mum, Dad

Thanks for doing the things I'm so rubbish at doing for me. My car loves you, as does my laundry basket. And thanks for being epic grandparents to my babies.

Thanks so much for reading, everyone. It means the world to me.

Your forever starts today. Make it count.

VICKI JAMES

ABOUT THE AUTHOR

Vicki James is a teenage girl stuck inside a much older body, and she refuses to grow up because that's just boring. With a ridiculous obsession for Rocky, Jax Teller, and Jamie Fraser, all she wishes to do is introduce the world to unforgettably flawed yet lovable characters like them. Vicki currently lives in Yorkshire, England, with her husband and two sons. Having had a strong passion for stories from a young age, she credits her love of literature to her Grandma Bess who taught her that you don't need a lot of money to travel to different worlds, experience new places, and live a thousand lives. When she's not listening to music or writing, she's usually at the gym pretending to workout.

She currently writes on her own as Vicki James, as well as writing the Babylon MC Series alongside her good friend Lou Stock.

Prior to 2019, Vicki James was better known as Victoria L. James before she concentrated on her current path. If you've read a book under the VLJ brand, please be aware that they are one and the same person.

Visit my website: www.vickijamesbooks.com/

Join my group

facebook.com/groups/1612818628945379

amazon.com/author/vickijames
instagram.com/vickijamesbooks
facebook.com/vickijamesauthor
goodreads.com/vickijamesauthor
bookbub.com/authors/vicki-james
TikTok.com/@vickijamesauthor

BOOKS BY VICKI

Natexus Series
Let Him Go
Let Him Stay
To Want Her
To Hold Her

Babylon MC Series
Without Consequence
Without Mercy
Without Truth
Without Shame
Without Forever

Gods of Rock Series
Cherry Beats
Dirty Rock
Ghost Note

Stand-alones
A Girl Like Lilac
The Trouble With Izzy
The Only Exception